Comrades

COMRADES

Bill Douglas

faber and faber
LONDON · BOSTON

First published in 1987
by Faber and Faber Limited
3 Queen Square London WC1N 3AU

Photoset and printed in Great Britain by
Redwood Burn Limited, Trowbridge, Wiltshire

British Library Cataloguing in Publication Data

Douglas, Bill
Comrades.
I. Title
822'.914   PR6054.O82/

ISBN 0–571–14947–2

For in and out, above, about, below,
'Tis nothing but a Magic Shadow-show,
Play'd in a Box whose Candle is the Sun,
Round which we Phantom Figures come and go.

The Rubáiyát of Omar Khayyám
translated by Edward FitzGerald

Arise, men of Britain and take your stand! Rally
round the standard of Liberty, or for ever lay
prostrate under the iron hand of your land and
money-mongering taskmasters!

George Loveless
Tolpuddle, August 1837

CHARACTERS

Principals

GEORGE LOVELESS (37)
Betsy (38) his wife
Hetty (5) their child
JAMES LOVELESS (25) brother of George
Sarah, his wife
THOMAS STANFIELD (44) known as Old Stanfield
Diana (40) his wife, sister of George and James Loveless
JOHN STANFIELD (21) their son, known as Young Stanfield
Elizabeth or Elvi (16) their elder daughter
Charity (7) their younger daughter
JAMES BRINE (20) later married Elvi Stanfield
Joseph (10) his brother
Mrs Brine (50) their widowed mother
John Hammett, a carpenter
Bridget, his pregnant wife
JAMES HAMMETT (22) his brother, unmarried

*LANTERNIST (all asterisked roles are played by one performer)

Dorset

Servant Girl
FRAMPTON
VICAR
Edward Legg
Foreman
Clerk
Blonde-haired girl
Dark-haired girl
SAILOR
*Sergeant Bell
MRS WETHAM
*Mr Wetham
MR PITT
*Diorama Showman
Two Gentleman Farmers
Constable
*Usher
*Wollaston
*Ranger
Gaoler
*Tramp

Machine-breakers, soldiers, villagers, members of Frampton's family and household, congregations, agricultural labourers, children, gypsy musicians, itinerant performers, stagehands, coachmen, townspeople, etc.

Australia

*Captain
THE FOP
Charlie
LONE ABORIGINE
Registrar
MRS CARLYLE
*McCallum
CONVICT ('NED LUDD')
McCallum's woman
Bertie, a guard
Digger
Official at burial
*Silhouettist
MR NORFOLK
Flower, his daughter
*Mad Photographer
*Witch
Auctioneer
Woman in white
Police Officer

Convicts, guards, officials, Aborigines, sailors, sentry, the Fop's followers, sheep herdsmen, crowd, etc.

NOTE

The published script of *Comrades* is almost wholly taken from the shooting script dated August 1984, which in turn was based very closely upon the original screenplay written in 1980. For ease of reading, all technical directions have been omitted. Some re-ordering of shots and scenes has taken place in order to correspond to the finished film, but a number of other scenes are retained here that do not appear in the film. All had been shot and edited but were later discarded under pressure to make the film shorter. Improvised dialogue and the words of songs have been added.

The blinding white circle of light that is the sun.

A cloud drifts swiftly by revealing the moon.

Now the sun and moon like sisters in the sky. Then gradually a sense of movement, infinitesimal: the moon going towards the sun, the sun coming towards the moon. A feeling of the impending eclipse.

Sudden lightning journey through space, like a chariot of fire through the heavens, a gigantic tumbling down towards the earth.

Twelve men, all dressed in women's clothing with homemade weapons in their hands, spread out across a field, are static for a moment, but only for a moment, as brief as a breath held.

Sudden shattering of glass and an oath.

A hammer dangles in a hand like a pendulum before making a frenzied motion through the air

and down to smash machinery.

The men dressed in women's clothing wield the weapons

while others down their strength on a crowbar.

The threshing machine starts grinding, causing the grain to spew out in all directions. Friction, sparks, sudden flame.

Slack rope jerked taut.

A stallion rears up, sensing danger.

The horses' hoofs approaching.

Instantly all hell is let loose as the men collide with fifteen soldiers on horseback in an acceleration of bodies. Fists meet truncheons meet scalps meet groins

runs blood.

A man runs forward with a burning torch

comes to meet a haystack

and lights up the old Lanternist's alarmed face. He considers the turmoil beneath him, distant, muted, transformed, like ants in a terrifying nightmare.

I

He stands on the hillside, separate, held, before

receding diagonally across the figure of the Giant of Cerne Abbas. He disappears with speed over the brow of the hill.

Title: COMRADES

The village, deserted and seemingly immune to the ringing of a handbell.

Subtitle: A LANTERNIST'S ACCOUNT OF THE TOLPUDDLE MARTYRS AND WHAT BECAME OF THEM

Rain blinds the Lanternist, plays havoc with him. He drags his smock up from behind him to shelter his lantern. He stands there shouting:

LANTERNIST: Galanty show, galanty show!

He cups his hands to his mouth, turns and calls out:

LANTERNIST: See John Gilpin make his ride, only a penny.

But the place remains deserted.

LANTERNIST: If you haven't got a penny, a halfpenny will do. If you haven't got a halfpenny, God bless you.

He turns and adds an additional enticement:

LANTERNIST: Straight from London.

He looks demoralized. He turns again, hearing a carriage and pair.

Like a phantom carriage it charges down the village street.

A solitary lighted window in the village turns to darkness.

The shadow of the carriage, the horses' hoofs raised in a threatening gesture, descends on the Lanternist who looks alarmed.

The carriage sweeps towards the hill, while the Lanternist quickly comes from behind, taking note. Ahead of him the carriage disappears on the ascent.

When we next see it, it is empty, with the two horses snuffling in the night air. In the background, through the trees, the house, wellnigh impenetrable, is merrily lit up.

There is a young servant girl framed in a lighted doorway. She is listening to the Lanternist say:

LANTERNIST: A show for the family, comical pictures of every description and colour.

There is a sudden clacking sound as he withdraws one of his chromatropes

to display it against the lamplight. He moves it round and round.

LANTERNIST: Endless rollicking laughter. Tell your master.

SERVANT GIRL: I can ask.

As she turns, she glances at

his feet standing in a pool of wet. We hear her go.

We watch the play of her shadow as it moves beyond the blinds. Judging by the number of windows it is a sizeable place, in contrast to the dwellings of the village. Through a window, in the lamplight, we see the shadows of figures – Mr Frampton and a gentleman farmer – at a table playing cards. There is something very refined and delicate about the shapes.

Frampton comes to a window and looks out. The silence is broken by the sound of a dog growling. This gives way to snarling as if it had something between its teeth. The dog barks ferociously. We hear a scampering, the jangle of the Lanternist's belongings. Finally there is only a high-pitched whimper, then silence. Frampton's expressionless face, staring. He moves away, letting a curtain fall into place.

The harvest moon. The Lanternist passes in silhouette.

He approaches the open window of George's house.

A hand making shadows on the wall.

A child's face, mouth open in wonder, watching.

The Lanternist is outside the window making mysterious hand movements by the light of the moon.

The shadow of his hand appears on the wall in the shape of a bird.

Hetty, the bright-eyed child, looks mesmerized.

George Loveless hears the Lanternist going into the distance calling:

LANTERNIST: Oh, oh, the lantern show, only a penny. You pay for the entertainment, the news is free. North. East. West. South. All the news is free.

The last words carry an emphasis.

Betsy glances up from her mending.

She prods a potato out of the fire. She snatches it into her apron.

Betsy leaves the house, clutching the potato in her apron. She walks along the muddy road.

As she turns a corner, she looks this way and that, sees what she wants and disappears from sight.

Hetty's face appears round a corner, wide-eyed, watching.

Some distance away, the Lanternist has an audience of two other villagers besides Betsy. He is witnessed as through the child's eyes, as a dumb-show with a strong play towards the melodramatic. When he moves it is to indicate something 'over there'. Like the showman he is, he relives the battle between the military and the machine-breakers, seeming to live and die a hundred times.

In Hetty's mind even the drums of battle are having their fling.

George leads his family along the street. They step into the sunlight. As he passes some of the houses, whether their doors are open or shut, he gives four friendly knocks in his own distinctive manner.

Hetty scampers on towards the house of James and Sarah Loveless.

She runs straight in the open door and makes for

James for the big hug she is used to expecting. There is a giggle of delight as he swings her in the air.

Sarah is watching them.

SARAH: Children become you.

James lets the excited child down and she scampers off. He doesn't respond to Sarah. It is clearly a subject he prefers to avoid.

SARAH: When can we have one of our own?

She comes to him and puts her head against his shoulder.

JAMES: How could we manage?

SARAH: I know times are bad . . .

When she turns to face him her eyes look sad.

SARAH: But I'm not getting any younger.

James smiles understanding. He hugs her.

JAMES: We are the most beautiful people in the whole world.

She laughs at his vanity.

JAMES: It's true.

She is quiet now in the thought that what they have is good.

James and Sarah come through the door of the Stanfields' house, greeting Old Stanfield and members of the family.

Diana tends the griddle of freshly baked rolls at the fire. Young Stanfield pinches a taste. It appears to be too hot for his mouth to handle. Diana laughs as much as to say 'serves you right'.

Elvi is busy stirring the cauldron of tea. She dips in the cups and as one by one they are withdrawn Betsy carries them away. There is a hustle and bustle going on as the family take their places round the table.

Charity is sitting between James and George. She hears her mother speak:

> DIANA: Do you know, when I was a little girl, I always had to sit between those two.

Charity is looking up at her mother as if she finds it hard to believe she was ever such a thing as a little girl like herself. Her mother says sadly:

> DIANA: Nothing changes.

Elvi is far far away in a dream world of her own. She is hypnotized by

James and Sarah playing their fingers game, an intertwining intimate thing. They appear to be as lost in their private world as Elvi is in hers. Then suddenly James catches

Elvi who averts her eyes.

Diana places the largest roll of all before Old Stanfield at the head of the table. It is her way of expressing her real fondness for him. Perhaps the gesture embarrasses him somewhat for he clears his throat to say grace.

There is a feeling of simple unity where they sit round the table.

> OLD STANFIELD: Dear Lord, we humbly beseech thee to accept our gratitude for this our daily bread . . .

The food on the table. There doesn't appear to be much more than bread.

> OLD STANFIELD: Give us the goodness of heart to share whatever we have in remembrance of thee.

> ALL: Amen.

He sits and they eat in silence.

A golden chalice and plate on the altar.

An elaborate stained-glass window with the sun streaming through. The sun's rays lead us to the Vicar, now dominating the pulpit. The opening text is read from the Bible.

> VICAR: Proverbs 14. In all labour there is profit: but the talk of the lips tendeth only to penury. The poor is hated even of his own neighbour: but the rich hath many friends.

In one and the same gesture he closes the Bible and bows to

Frampton who has the look of one in absolute accordance with

7

the written word. Occupying an enclosure with him are his wife and six children together with members of their household, perhaps an aged parent, children's maid, coachman, foreman and servant girl, all in their Sunday best.

We see Edward Legg sitting meekly with his twin daughters.

> VICAR: In all labour there is profit, and it behoves us to accept our lot in life and to work for our reward. Let us never forget that our Lord humbled Himself for all our sakes . . .

We have been moving among the congregation and come to rest on John Hammett and his pregnant wife, Bridget.

> VICAR: . . . to be born of the wife of a carpenter on this poor earth. Let us strive to excel in the role we are born to, remembering we are all beholden to our Maker.

We now see the entire congregation from the rear of the church.

> VICAR: God the Father, in His infinite wisdom, created large men and small, white men and black, rich men and poor, wise men and fools.

On closer inspection we sense that one member of the congregation, young Brine, can't stomach much more.

> VICAR: And we should not dare to presume to question His wisdom. The talk of the lips tendeth only to penury. Abjure it. Abjure it.

The Vicar's lips, which we see now carry a warning.

> VICAR: Hold fast to that which we know and have learned to value, the natural order of things, tried and tested down the ages of man. It is not mere chance that in all living things there is law and order.

The Vicar is brought down to earth when there appears to be a slight commotion. His attention is torn between his notes and what he sees.

> VICAR: There are enemies of the church – dissenters – who speak together blasphemously . . .

Somewhere in the congregation Brine is on his feet, much to the consternation of Mrs Brine and his younger brother Joseph. With looks more than words, he and his mother appear to be having a struggle for authority, which in turn distracts the congregation around them. As Brine finally breaks away, the Vicar's voice rises as if to stop him, but he seems to lose his place or is so angry that he splutters and can get no more words out.

9

VICAR: ... tampering with God's work, challenging our traditions. Be not drawn by the Devil's smile. Abjure it. The talk of the lips ... The poor is hated ... Let us now sing ... the hymn ...

Sound of the organ hurrying in, forcing the congregation to its feet, though some are still turning away to watch Brine disappear down the aisle and out the door. As they start to sing, their lack of unity at odds with the urgency of the accompanying organ, the Vicar appears following in the direction Brine has taken and steps outside.

Across a stretch of grass, Brine progresses with a sense of purpose. As he goes the sound of the organ and disjointed voices are overtaken by the encroaching sound of the Methodist hymn, which by contrast is a rich raw singing without accompaniment.

VOICES: Come all who would to glory go,
And leave this world of sin and woe;
Forsake your sins without delay,
Believe, and you shall win the day.

The building of a simple Methodist chapel. Brine hovers in front of the place, disappearing up one side and back down the other. He enters the way a stranger might and as quiet as a mouse.

VOICES: We'll win the day, we'll win the day,
Though death and hell obstruct the way;
We only need to watch and pray
And then we're sure to win the day.

Inside the atmosphere is bright. Everything is plain and simple, both the place and the people. At the end of their hymn, George leads the congregation in prayer:

GEORGE: Give us the vision Lord to see beyond the narrow confines of the field to the great and infinite glory of the world beyond. Help us to stretch ourselves to the full extent of our being that we may be one with all men, neither master nor servant, before thine eyes. Amen.

VOICES: Amen.

George opens his eyes.

The congregation fills the small chapel and watches George with much affection. Brine can be seen quite clearly standing at the

back conspicuous because of his exhilarated smile.

GEORGE: Jesus has given us many blessings. And one of these my friends is to smile.

We notice Charity glancing over her shoulder.

Brine lets her take him by the hand and lead him to mingle with the rest of the congregation. He joins Old Stanfield's family, alongside Elvi. Charity squeezes herself to another place beside Young Stanfield.

GEORGE: I love every new day. But Sundays are best of all, for how good it is to see all of you joining together. During the coming weeks we shall call upon the services of my good brother James.

James Loveless stands up enthusiastically.

JAMES: Thank you. I would like to talk about comradeship. About the disciples who laid down their work to follow in the path of truth. I look forward to your good attendance.

SARAH: Praise the Lord.

Hetty, sitting between Betsy and Sarah, whispers excitedly in Sarah's ear. Her mother shushes her to pay attention.

GEORGE: No planning ahead would be complete without calling on our good friend and neighbour, Tom Stanfield. Tom?

They all look up at Old Stanfield.

OLD STANFIELD: As well as reading the word of God, I will leave part of my time open for anyone to approach me with a subject for discussion.

Charity finds herself nudged by her brother to put forward a suggestion but she shakes her head rapidly.

OLD STANFIELD: All our troubles are shared by Jesus. So please come forward and don't be shy.

As he is about to sit down he adds:

OLD STANFIELD: It is worth bearing in mind, a grief shared is a smaller grief.

As Brine listens to Old Stanfield he appears quite moved. Finally George is heard saying:

GEORGE: I see we have a stranger in our midst. I'm glad you had the temerity to enter, for now we know who trod the grass these Sundays past.

The congregation laughs good naturedly, some looking round to see who the stranger might be. Brine looks suitably bashful, but even more embarrassed when Elvi puts an arm around his neck and hugs him.

GEORGE: Welcome, lad.

Sound of the organ. Grinding carriage wheels through muddy dirt.

The congregation emerges from the church to mingle with the chapel congregation as one community on the village green. George Loveless, James Loveless, Old Stanfield, Young Stanfield and Brine are under the tree which occupies the centre of the place, in a little circle facing inwards. The carriage we have just seen takes to the hill while a horseman gallops towards us. In the distance, going up through the village itself, a horse and buggy. There are two carriages left in the vicinity of the church, one already on the move towards the hill.

Frampton, his family and household, are coming along the path from church. Frampton holds back and walks a few steps away in company with the Vicar. In muted conversation they go back towards the church, then turn and come back towards us. On his way Frampton looks to his left pointedly towards

the circle of men under the tree, who are completely wrapped up in themselves.

As his family gathers around the carriage, Frampton shakes hands with the Vicar, and moves off to join

Mrs Frampton and a daughter, who carries a doll dressed just like herself.

Mrs Brine has her eye on the Vicar, who appears to be coming in her direction. One or two people offer their hand to the Vicar as he passes so that it looks more like a goodwill tour than Mrs Brine's face would have us believe. However, when he reaches her, the Vicar passes her by. We go with him till he meets up with Legg, who is standing separately with his two children. The Vicar offers Legg his hand, then places it on the head of one of the children.

A carriage passes revealing an ashen Mrs Brine leaning to whisper in her son Joseph's ear. He leaves her and crosses the road.

Joseph approaches the tree on the village green. He goes to tug at his brother's jacket. Brine looks put out, probably embarrassed to be thought tied to his mother's apron strings. He moves away from the circle, gesticulating. He throws out his palm as if to say 'what do you want?' then turns the same hand back to the group, 'I'm with my friends'. He finishes by putting his hands together pleading prayer, 'I'm sorry'. Joseph ends by thumping him and he retaliates with a kick.

Mrs Brine, her back to us, marches towards her homestead. Very soon Joseph runs after her, and we have the feeling she is the dominant figure in her household.

John Hammett and Bridget his wife stroll across the green. Where John's face lights up, Bridget's looks worried. After touching her arm as if to reassure her,

he goes towards the men under the tree and shakes hands with them.

Bridget looks as though some sixth sense is telling her something, and she whispers to herself for the Lord to be with us. Suddenly the Vicar appears at her side.

At the Hammetts' house there is a knock on the door in George's distinctive manner.

John and Bridget look up, like an apology, from their carpentry. Both at this moment are as rigid as statues. Suddenly at a flapping signal from John's hand, they burst into a hive of activity, hiding away the evidence of their work. The sound of knocking comes again.

John is now sitting erect in a chair as if nothing untoward has happened. We hear Bridget open the door.

BRIDGET: George. Come in. We thought it was the Vicar.

Hammett turns from his sleep, bedded down in the straw, unshaven and resentful at being woken.

HAMMETT: I wouldn't trust the Vicar with a fart.

GEORGE: Forgive me, my dear chap. I had no idea we had the pleasure of your company.

We see George at the head of the table with Bridget and John on either side. John follows George's glance to

telltale shavings at the foot of the drawn green curtain.

George stretches out to join Bridget and John's hands.

GEORGE: John. Bridget. My dear friends. Are your labours

14

more important than the Sabbath day?

Hammett pulls the curtain aside revealing his grubby self, stretching and scratching and smelling his own sweat from 'neath his armpits.

GEORGE: We all need a day of rest. Maybe your brother has the right idea though it pains me to admit it.

Hammett grabs up his hat

and stomps out banging the door behind him.

George smiles tolerantly.

JOHN: I wish times was different, George, when we could have back the respect we give to others.

Bridget looks up as we hear the sound of John moving and drawing the curtain fully back.

JOHN: If you'll forgive me then, George.

George nods and we hear John resume his work.

JOHN: Mr Frampton demands they be sat in this very week.

We isolate one of the finished chairs.

George is very moved.

GEORGE: They are a work of great beauty. When we create with our hands such harmony, God is truly present.

We examine the six chairs, their appearance looking somewhat incongruous in this wretched place. We trace the delicate workmanship, the sheer symmetry and fineness of them, upholstered with Bridget's handiwork on the seats.

George takes hold of Bridget's hand, considers it with gentleness, kisses it and places it against her pregnant belly, holding it there. Bridget sitting beside George buries her face in his shoulder.

BRIDGET: He's been awake the whole night through.

George strokes her head. Then she looks up and gives a beautiful smile. George looks about him

at the rain dripping through the ceiling.

John is deeply involved in his carpentry and Bridget returns to her work by his side. We can hear George pacing the floor.

Then catch him standing by a rear window where the rain is hitting the glass. He sighs a deep sigh.

GEORGE: Why don't you ask for more payment?

JOHN: Because, George, if they don't like it, they'll find someone else.

George continues looking out of the window.

GEORGE: Yes.

He wipes the mist from the pane with a single sweep of the hand.

GEORGE: But supposing all you carpenters were to ask for more.

The carpenter and his wife look at one another in silence. John glances up

to catch George giving him a wink. Then George looks out of the window. He hides himself, suggesting something outside. He is in a playful mood.

Out in the yard, Charity is oblivious to the drizzle. She is on her haunches delving among the cast-off wood shavings for any little bits and pieces that take her fancy. These she rescues into her sagging skirt. She doesn't hear the gentle tapping on the glass at first. She is too entranced by her finds.

At the window, George looks highly amused. He taps again.

The child glances up. Suddenly there is the sound of a clack from the door latch

and he has the little girl running for her life. But brave enough to snatch for any fallen piece.

George is hard at work in the fields, hedging and ditching. As he digs he finds what might well be part of an old Roman vessel. He looks intrigued with it, turning it this way and that. He throws it away and continues digging.

Brine is ploughing, with his small brother Joseph leading the pair of horses. Walking through the wet soil, his boots are thick with earth and he stumbles from time to time.

Old Stanfield is picking up stones from the ploughed field, which he puts into the basket or bag on his back. There are others, including women, in the background doing likewise. We sense that he is ready to collapse from the strain of constantly stooping.

Young Stanfield is muck-spreading. With his fork, he makes a patchwork across the field. The Foreman passes in his wagon and Young Stanfield catches his ever-watchful eye.

James Loveless is sowing seed with the aid of a seed drill, while others in the background do the same. On an impulse he stops and looks over his shoulder.

Hammett is on his own, hoeing, in a field of half-grown corn. There is a scarecrow clad in cast-off gentry clothing with a bright red neckerchief. He looks around to check that he is unobserved and deftly removes the neckerchief.

A line of pigeons croaking in the rafters of the barn. It is pay day.

FOREMAN: Abbott.

The men are all standing inside the barn, about twenty-three of them, stooping wearily from their labours.

FOREMAN: Arscott.

Behind the desk the Clerk is quite sprightly-looking, very much

17

from the town. He has charge of the wages and a ledger, while the Foreman stands by his side.

FOREMAN: Brown.

A workman steps forward, he marks an 'X' in the ledger in the space indicated by the manicured fingernail, accepts his money and goes.

FOREMAN: Buxton.

YOUNG STANFIELD: Sir?

The Clerk winces.

YOUNG STANFIELD: Far be it for my friend here to seek priority over his comrades . . .

CLERK: Oh dear.

YOUNG STANFIELD: Nor does he wish to take yourself too obviously to task. But, as I understand the alphabet, does not the 'i' in Brine precede the 'o' in Brown and indeed the 'u' in Buxton?

Young Stanfield has affected part of his speech and his friend

Brine is busy trying to put in his own words. They are like a comedy duo.

CLERK: In time, comrade, in good time.

The number of workmen has now diminished to seventeen.

FOREMAN: Hammett.

The Clerk turns to one side as if something offensive has reached his nose. He surreptitiously removes a fleck of dirt from his hands, as Hammett takes his money.

Hammett walks away putting up seven fingers and shaking his head, disgruntled.

FOREMAN: Lost a finger have you, Hammett? Or is it just you can't count?

Hammett puts up the missing finger in an insulting gesture. The men laugh, and there is a peremptory call for:

FOREMAN: Legg.

We watch Legg in profile as he signs, takes his money and leaves.

FOREMAN: Loveless.

Comically enough both George and James Loveless step out. But the Clerk's voice stops them in their tracks.

CLERK: George first, James following.

GEORGE: Let my brother go first for I have not reconciled.

CLERK: Not reconciled what?

GEORGE: My conscience.

The Clerk winces. The men that are left nod in agreement.

The number of workers has reduced to eight.

FOREMAN: Stanfield.

YOUNG STANFIELD: Do you call father or son?

Old Stanfield touches his son in a pacifying gesture and goes before him.

Old Stanfield signs his 'X'. This column in the ledger is now almost an uninterrupted line. The Clerk's fingers concealing eight coins come to leave them at the edge of the desk.

OLD STANFIELD: I think there must be some mistake. We should be getting nine shillings not eight.

CLERK: There has been no mistake, Mr Stanfield. You must

19

take it or leave it.

Old Stanfield shakes his head as if he were expecting trouble.

The Clerk hints at a smile behind his hand. Just then a pigeon dropping lands on his sleeve. He jumps up in a rage.

The Foreman helps him to move the desk further back and, self-satisfied, he resumes his seat. But to no avail for another dropping lands immediately on his ledger.

Finally there is only Brine left.

FOREMAN: Brine.

It appears Brine is slow to move for the Clerk is now heard to call out with greater emphasis:

CLERK: Brine. Will you sign? We haven't all day.

The Clerk sits there holding out a pen.

But Brine is in no hurry. He stands against the wall, glowering, like a rabbit caught in a trap.

That night George comes swiftly from his house. Gathering his garment to him against the wind, he hurries towards a window. He knocks four distinct times, then moves away. After a moment we can hear him knock on another window.

We come upon James Loveless. He moves away from his wife, revealing her nakedness. His hand trails along the length of her arm. She reaches out to him.

Sarah clutches at his hand, means to hold on. But it goes leaving her wanton. She turns away, her hand folding itself pitying to her face.

James lowers his shirt over his face, revealing an expression of total determination. He shows no response to the sound of smothered whimpers. He splashes water from a bowl to his face, bathing himself in it.

The sleeping Mrs Brine does not open her eyes at the window being knocked. Gradually we hear sounds of movement in the room.

Although we can barely make him out in the half-light we know it is Brine who is leaving. He closes the door quietly behind him and we can hear his footsteps going away. His mother comes to bolt the door on him.

George is seen coming down the village street. James comes

hurrying after him, followed by Brine. They are joined by others coming out of doors. In no time at all the number has multiplied. There is a sense of purposefulness in their movement.

George is standing on the bank of a stream, when a sound like a bird comes to him. He turns.

His brother James is at an upstairs window. He makes a signal with a lamp, that all is ready.

George splashes through the water.

Through the trees, a figure striding through the gloom. We can see the lantern humped up on his back.

George hurries the Lanternist up the stairs outside the Stanfields' house and through a door. Within the room there is a lighted window, the only one emitting light. There is clearly something of great portent going on.

Some of the local women are waiting by the edge of the field early next day. Gradually they are met up with their menfolk who take from them what might be their breakfast. Off they go back across the field with their cloth bundles, as the women disperse. Brine appears still to be waiting for his to come. Having waited long enough, he glances stealthily over his shoulder.

Brine approaches the door to his cottage. He tries the latch, it won't open.

BRINE: Mother?

No answer. Then:

BRINE: I'm hungry. Let me in.

He shivers with cold, is beside himself wondering what to do. Finally he goes away. No sooner has he gone than there is a light visible through the window. Mrs Brine opens the door. She comes out staring after him.

Brine is moving along the path between the fields. He looks deep in thought. He glances to either side of him looking increasingly awkward.

The bush quivers slightly as if invaded by a rabbit.

It is in fact Brine. He is snuggled out of sight, rubbing the earth

from a turnip. He bites into it with the ferocity of a dog. There is no sound save the squelching and spitting of a terrible hunger. It must be a good feeling to be able to eat, for it has made him cry.

Barely a foot away is a conspicuous gap in the furrows of a turnip field. Brine's hand stretches out like a dislocated thing to replace what is left of the turnip. The field looks suitably back to normal.

On the village green, Charity has all the little decorative bits of carving displayed in a semi-circle while she crouches behind them. Her customer, young Joseph Brine, considers them.

CHARITY: You mustn't touch.

JOSEPH: What price are they?

CHARITY: Ten a penny.

Joseph thinks about that.

JOSEPH: That isn't a bargain.

Charity looks quite put out.

CHARITY: They're a bargain at twice the price.

Joseph is on his way. We hear Charity calling after him.

22

CHARITY: A dozen then.

Joseph turns around. He says almost apologetically:

JOSEPH: I only have a halfpenny.

We eye the coin like a jewel in Joseph's hand.

CHARITY: I don't really sell halfpenny's worth.

Then with sudden animation of generosity:

CHARITY: But as a special favour to you . . .

She selects her pieces.

CHARITY: Five a halfpenny.

We can see her grabbing hand, hear the coin join with a merry clink the others in her lap.

Poor Joseph doesn't look too happy.

Compared with the rest of the merchandise she has selected the most uninteresting pieces.

That night, the whole Stanfield family – Old Stanfield, Young Stanfield, Diana, Elvi and Charity – are lying abed. They lie head to toe on the hay across the floor. Their visitor Brine lifts himself up on to an elbow with his eyes wide open

for Elvi, who is turned away. We would think she was unaware of her admirer if it wasn't that her fingers are crossed.

Next to Elvi's feet lies Charity, who proceeds to slip the coins that she has taken between Elvi's toes.

The two lads are taking a jaunty walk, Young Stanfield with his hand clasping Brine's shoulder. Whatever they are talking about we can't make out, but it has an easy come easy go feeling about it in keeping with an evening stroll.

Two girls, one blonde-haired and the other dark, are leaning back, arms linked, against a fence. They appear to be gazing into space until one looks to the other in a knowing way. The two boys are alongside, but separate and with their backs to us. They appear motionless until Young Stanfield in one fell swoop of bravado leaps the fence.

YOUNG STANFIELD: C'mon, Briney.

Like an athlete born, Brine sizes up the height of the fence. He dashes forward as if to outdo Young Stanfield then merely skirts the obstacle. The girls look the other way. The two boys marvel

23

at one another's masculinity. Young Stanfield hoists himself up on the fence, arms fully extended, then down again, dropping himself right beside the ear of the dark-haired one.

YOUNG STANFIELD: What you doing this afternoon then?

No answer.

YOUNG STANFIELD: Shall we go blackberry picking? A bit of blackberry picking in the woods there?

The girls smother a smile.

YOUNG STANFIELD: What you do with blackberries, you squash them all up, rub them all over your face, and then you lick the juice off. Be nice, eh?

There is no sound to be heard, just the birds twittering. Brine, sensing a further display of manliness is called for, decides to stride the fence. Tapping Young Stanfield on the shoulder so that all eyes may be on him, he hoists himself up only to find the entire fence giving way beneath him.

The girls explode into helpless laughter. Unimpressed, they move off, followed by an undaunted Young Stanfield. Left behind, poor Brine appears the worse for wear. He hobbles after them.

Across the field, the two boys are on the move. Way ahead of them the two girls are patiently strolling. When the boys reach an opening into the woods, the one nudges the other for them to disappear.

They re-emerge and arrive at a point where they expect to confront the girls. The girls are nowhere to be seen but we can hear them giggling in the distance.

Brine and Young Stanfield press forward through the trees and as they go they pass an opening in a folly where they stop and retrace a few steps.

Round the wall we take a peep.

The blonde-haired girl is waiting at one side, while the dark-haired girl appears to be chatting effervescently, but to whom?

Gradually revealed is Hammett. He finds an excuse to touch the girl's hair by moving it off her shoulder. She in turn touches the hair he has moved. He takes a red neckerchief and puts it round her neck.

The Foreman brings his wagon to a halt outside the Hammetts' house.

Standing at the door, John Hammett looks on protectively as if he were losing an only child.

One of the carpenter's elegant chairs is being hoisted into the wagon where it joins the others.

George is dozing at the table while Betsy is clearing the ashes. She looks across the room a couple of times and then goes to close the door. She goes on with her work.

The Foreman ropes the chairs, securing them with a knot. He goes to tend the horse then climbs into his seat.

Hearing the sound of the approaching vehicle, George opens his eyes. He gets to his feet and goes out.

George, all arms flailing, brings the wagon to a halt. The horse snuffles.

Betsy is sitting at the hearth fretting. Her hands are covering her face.

BETSY: Dear God, teach him not to think. Help him to accept things as they are. Don't let him question things . . .

But barely a moment later she adds:

BETSY: Well, not too much.

George feels the carving on the back of one of the chairs.

GEORGE: Handsome bit of work.

The Foreman considers the bounty behind him and shakes his head.

FOREMAN: You'd have to get yourself a new pair of breeches before you could sit in one of them.

He laughs. George nods in agreement.

GEORGE: What's his asking price?

FOREMAN: Pound apiece.

GEORGE: Know how long it takes him?

The Foreman thinks a bit.

GEORGE: Two weeks a chair. Getting on.

George considers the Foreman for a moment, then tentatively:

GEORGE: What would you say to your trying to up the price a bit?

The Foreman looks momentarily taken aback. He extends his hand in the direction he has come and makes to speak but George cuts him short.

GEORGE: I'll take full responsibility.

The Foreman considers the situation.

FOREMAN: I can ask . . .

GEORGE: Good man.

George is so pleased he leaps on to the seat beside the Foreman. Then they are off with George shouting:

GEORGE: I'll to the top of the hill with you.

With a lash of the whip the wagon takes the hill and disappears over the crest, regaled by the sun.

But it comes to nothing, for the next thing we know the chairs have been replaced by the carpenter's doorway.

There is a pile of wood shavings on the table.

Charity has her face to the wall. One of her hands is seen splayed out. She is sobbing. Diana's voice is heard saying:

DIANA: Come.

Charity remains.

Diana is waiting inside her chair with her hand held out.

DIANA: Come to me.

Then she holds the child in an embrace.

DIANA: I'm not angry with you.

She moves back the child's face to reassure her.

DIANA: You see . . .

She thinks to say the right things.

DIANA: If we get something for nothing in this world, it means someone else may have to suffer. Now that's not a good thing, is it?

Charity shakes her head against her mother's stomach. Diana smiles warmly.

DIANA: It's quite simple really, you know. We only have to love one another to know what we must do.

When Charity opens her eyes on her mother it is with a searching look.

Diana smiles as if there was nothing at all complicated about life. If anyone holds the secret in her eyes she does.

Elvi walks along the road with Brine. She goes towards the cottage alone. Before going in, she gives an anxious little look back at

Brine, who hovers around awkwardly.

Inside the Brines' cottage, Elvi puts the halfpenny on the table before her.

ELVI: Forgive Charity. She meant no harm.

Mrs Brine gives her a calculating look and glances past her towards the window.

Elvi in turn peers slightly over Mrs Brine's shoulder.

Joseph is hovering anxiously in the corner, with his hands glued over his ears and his head shaking.

MRS BRINE: He's a good lad. He's not perfect. He has his ups and downs like the rest of us. But . . .

Poor Joseph looks as though he will burst into tears.

Elvi, having a good heart, puts her hand to her lips and shakes her head.

MRS BRINE: He's been a good son to me.

Joseph chooses this moment to close the door behind him.

Mrs Brine laughs, seeing the funny side. She picks up the halfpenny due to her.

MRS BRINE: Who'd have sons?

Elvi, a little disconcerted, looks over her shoulder.

Brine can be seen outside the window pacing up and down, more like an expectant father than a likely suitor.

Brine and Elvi are strolling along the country road together. She looks at his serious face and laughs. He looks about himself.

BRINE: What's funny?

Elvi shakes her head and, unable to contain herself, doubles up.
It appears they are being followed by Joseph.

There is a sudden confrontation between Brine and his brother.

BRINE: Now get you back. You can't come with us. Go on,
get you back.

All Joseph does is to take a few steps on a straight line with
himself and stand there. He looks totally put out.

The two continue on their way, Elvi glancing back
sympathetically.

When they get to the river bank, Joseph is clutching Elvi's hand
and at a safe distance from Brine.

In the village, we see Young Stanfield in a huff outside his door.
After a minute he goes inside and bangs it shut.

Outside the carpenter's door wait the six elegant chairs. Hetty is
sitting on one of them, playing houses, making conversation
with an imaginary friend.

When we find George, he looks a different man. His face is
ashen, his body limp with sunken weariness. We hear the sound
of Betsy's voice.

We see her with her hand on the latch of the carpenter's door.
She laughs in reply to something said inside and with a final

'cheerio' she comes away. She passes behind George without giving him as much as a look, but her furious manner is perhaps heightened for his benefit. She snatches Hetty from the chair and rubs the seat where the child has been with the hem of her skirt.

She smacks her lightly on their way to her own door and goes inside, slamming it behind her. A moment later she opens the door again and stands there looking visibly upset. She looks at George searchingly for a moment before she finally goes inside, closing the door silently behind her.

We hear a latch go up, and see Bridget emerge through the carpenter's door. She is very full with child. She looks for a moment, then comes carrying a small cup in her hands. She watches while George drinks from the cup. When at last he can bring himself to face her

her reaction is to radiate a smile.

Up the hill they go, six men of Tolpuddle – George and James, Old Stanfield and Young, Brine and John Hammett – each of them carrying a chair. They break into song:

ALL: A poor man to labour believe me 'tis so
   To maintain his family is willing to go
   Either hedging or ditching to plough or to reap
   But how does he live on eight shillings a week?
   Eight shillings a week
   Eight shillings a week
   But how does he live on eight shillings a week?

As they become smaller across the landscape their voices become stronger as each one multiplies the others:

   So now to conclude and to finish my song
   May the times be much better before it's too long
   May every labourer be able to keep
   His children and wife on twelve shillings a week
   Twelve shillings a week
   Twelve shillings a week
   His children and wife on twelve shillings a week.

James Loveless scythes the corn and heaves.

His body on the turn glistens with sweat.

Scything again he pauses to wipe the perspiration from his

brow. Just then a sound of trotting reaches him, causing him to look.

In the distance, between the fields, we can see Frampton's carriage. It is open, revealing the family at leisure. Perhaps they are returning from a picnic. Beneath parasols children giggle delightedly.

It is twilight now and the workers are still back-bent across the fields. They have no identity these men, just hands, working away incessantly with the rhythm of machines.

Finally the entire landscape is dark but still they work, their bodies silhouetted by the lamps.

James has fallen asleep where he has been sitting, his body hanging by the armpits over the back of the chair. His scythe has slipped to lean against his knees. Sarah touches his hand gently.

SARAH: James . . .

But James simply shakes a weary head.

SARAH: You must come to bed.

James mutters something incoherent.

Sarah places the implement silently against the door.

In the early morning Sarah is out to the world.

Beside the closed door, the scythe is gone. James has gone back to work.

A lone sailor carrying his furlough pack on his shoulder is strolling along the deserted country road. He sways from side to side in an exaggerated way as if still on board ship. He seems to be on his own until the music starts. There is a distant tune of a sailor's hornpipe on a fiddle. The beat appears to be sending him up. It is slow and plodding in keeping with his rhythm. He stops. The music stops. He shields his eyes and squints at the horizon. Nothing. He continues at a quicker pace, the tune again keeping him company. The sailor stops once more. He bangs the side of his head to let the sea water out. From some way away come sounds of girlish laughter. The sailor breaks into a smile. There's no stopping him now. There is the promise of girls in his gait, the music in his blood.

Suddenly the sailor is on the village green, giving us the hornpipe. He is amazingly energetic and full of life-on-the-sea. The accompanying fiddle trebles and quadruples in time, and on and on he goes as if in flight. It is a virtuoso performance.

The village folk surrounding him catch his energy like a fever. It is there in their faces and hands as they clap and shout him on.

The gypsy fiddler can be seen driving his strings.

Hetty can be seen pulling on her mother's apron strings to be let up.

The sailor's feet at this moment are quite simply airborne.

Sitting alone on a fence, Elvi is a picture of absolute joy.

But Brine looks a little bit jealous.

As the hornpipe comes to an end, Elvi has her head inclined against her shoulder. Perhaps the sailor symbolizes for her worlds she will never see, for her eyes are suddenly full of longing.

The sailor continues on his way. A solitary being with only his thoughts to keep him company. He goes leaving a momentary emptiness behind.

Now on the village green the villagers themselves have joined in the dance. Amid a world of plenty the young women with laurels of corn in their hair dance with their young men in a devil-me-care. The children are getting in everyone's way but nobody seems to mind. For this is the Harvest Festival, and itinerant performers are here for their catch.

SERGEANT BELL: Roll up, roll up, for don't you know it's Sergeant Bell and his Royal Raree Show.

The pegleg old soldier is the owner of the peepshow. He is surrounded by excited children, oohing and aahing. He has the gift of the gab and keeps up a string of commentary to his pictures mostly in doggerel.

SERGEANT BELL: Highly instructive for lads and lasses, ideal for the gentry and the labouring classes.

Charity and Joseph come to peep into the lenses of the peepshow.

SERGEANT BELL: Come on, now don't hog it. Let the lady in.

A penny greases his palm and he clenches it.

Mrs Brine and the Vicar find themselves at neighbouring lenses.

SERGEANT BELL: Ah, there's the man of God.
    I've the very thing for you, sir.
    Jacob and Adam in the land of Nod.
    Now it's only a penny to take a look,
    to see the pictures from the Holy Book.
    Oh sir, I beg your pardon,
    it's Eve – without her clothes on – in the garden.

Sergeant Bell's hand pulls the string.

Mrs Brine lets out an 'ah'.

The Vicar puts an eye closer to the lens.

Inside his dark box is the jewel of his wares. But whatever the illustration may be, Sergeant Bell's monologue is at odds with the subject. His is a talent to persuade.

SERGEANT BELL: Roll up for Sergeant Bell and his Raree Show.

Only a penny to see the view.
See Nelson being defeated at the Battle of Waterloo.

His patter carries over another game of mystery and revelation as, just then, Frampton's carriage draws up for a look. The family don't emerge, just peer out of the windows.

SERGEANT BELL: A Raree Show's the thing for all the lads and lasses.
Be careful now, young chisellers, not to breathe on the glasses.

The wagon piled high stands testament to a successful harvest. The musicians pass by, revealing Brine and Young Stanfield who are dancing together to the amusement of the blonde- and dark-haired girls crowding perilously atop the wagon of corn. The boys pull them down by the legs to make them join in, much to the grievance of Hammett, who sticks his head up from the corn to see where they have gone.

He has been observed by James Loveless, who leans to whisper in George's ear. George follows the line of his gaze, but frowns and shakes his head very firmly.

Now George whispers in James's ear. James glances out, considers and shakes his head in disapproval. But George is already beckoning with his hand. He points 'yes, you' and sweeps forward with an upward curve of the arm.

Legg, who has been standing alone, comes forward.

George gives Legg a warm handshake as round the tree go the musicians.

We hear the clip-clip-clop of Frampton's carriage and see it moving off.

Somehow the word has spread for out of the crowd three or four others are approaching the tree. There is much shaking of hands. The gypsy band encircles the tree as if uniting them.

Somewhere at the top of the tree, amongst the branches, there is a spread of light.

And still the villagers are dancing, round and round, as if they hadn't a care in the world.

We see an escapologist and a juggler selling their talents. We can hear the magician promising to make the world disappear.

At sundown the musicians take to the hill to calls of goodbye.

The fiddler jigs his legs in response before ascending the crest.

The villagers wave from the bottom of the hill. They wait, listening to the last strains of the music, wait even after it has died, as if they are loath to let the good times pass.

The sunset follows the musicians over the crest of the hill.

At pay day there is a light drizzle, though the children are barefoot waiting outside the barn. There isn't much energy about them but this could be because they are hungry and wet. After a moment one of the workers walks out of the place. He takes no notice of the children nor they of him. We hear the names being called out from inside. One of the children scampers to get into her father's arms. He murmurs something about being too tired. The child, understanding nothing of this, insists. He barks at her. She cries, but up she goes. Hammett comes out of the barn, grim-faced. He stands incredulously and puts up his fingers to indicate 'seven' shillings only. He turns away momentarily

and signals again angrily 'yes, seven'. The place is totally silent.

The men are waiting under the tree as the last drips of rain are falling. They are gradually met up with by others carrying their children. Apart from an occasional nod they are as solemn as a funeral.

Old Stanfield is standing some way away at the side of the fields. The old boy has a faraway look in his eyes.

Charity looks up from his hand, sensitive to these things. She presses his hand gently against her young face.

Outside the house, Betsy plucks a leaf from a clump of weeds. She goes through the open door closing it behind her.

Inside, Hetty pulls up her shift revealing a blotch of red on her white skin. Betsy smoothes the weed over the spots. Every now and then she casts a glance across the room and eventually the child follows her gaze.

George is sitting at the table in a state of depression. There is no sound except for the wife putting the child to rights. Hetty wanders to the table. She stretches up her hands to take the open book George appears to have abandoned. Just as the child

is about to finger the paper George springs to life and crashes his hand down on it. The frightened child screams. There is a drawing of a skeleton with the words REMEMBER THINE END.

That night, lying in the darkened room, George's head is almost hidden inside his arms.

It is then that the insects come. They emerge through a crack in the wall, hordes of them, in a never-ending stream. It seems as if there is no place for them to go but forward.

They ooze out of the floorboards.

George's feet protrude through the straw like carvings.

Insects come from the centre of his book, or at least this is where we come upon them and it seems as if they had issued out of the very thing itself.

George digs a torch deep into the embers.

He moves the scorching thing over the wall.

A myriad of falling lights touch the floor and die.

A clump of women at the edge of the field. The child given to Bridget screams into life.

She is being attended to where she lies.

Seen upside down, the child's face, newly born.

Sarah, acting as a midwife, stirs a cauldron of water. Somewhere outside their house an argument ensues between John Hammett and his brother. Sarah glances up, looks anxiously across at Bridget's child, for the moment undisturbed. Then at Bridget herself who lies abed like a vision of death. Behind the door the words are becoming quite heated.

JOHN: If mother was alive to see what you've become.

HAMMETT: You leave our mother out of this, John Hammett.

JOHN: There's such a thing as responsibility.

HAMMETT: And what's so responsible about fathering a child when you can barely afford to make ends meet?

JOHN: Just who d'you think you are telling me what to do?

HAMMETT: Your brother, that's who.

JOHN: Let's get this straight. My first loyalty is to Bridget and the baby.

HAMMETT: I see, you want me out the way now there's an extra mouth to feed, is that it?

JOHN: That's a good idea. There's the road.

HAMMETT: I'm boss in my life, not you nor anyone else. I'll decide what I want to do where and when I want to do it.

Bridget manages an interior smile. Judging by the level of the voices, John appears to have wandered away. But Hammett makes up for that by shouting:

HAMMETT: That bloody baby has gone right to your head.

It is enough for Sarah. She crosses the floor to yank up a lethal shaft of wood. She charges towards the door.

However on opening it Sarah is met with total silence. Her warrior face beholds

an innocent-looking Hammett making up to the blonde- and dark-haired girls.

A shushing sound causes Sarah to turn.

An equally innocent John is pacing up and down with the newborn child in his arms.

Blossom and Decay, a *trompe-l'oeil* picture, in a shop window. This is Wetham's Print Shop in the town of Dorchester. Prints of one kind and another fill each of the windowpanes. There are no signs of people, just a gathering of sheep passing by with their monotonous mewing.

MRS WETHAM: What on earth is it?

Inside the shop, Mrs Wetham, wife of the proprietor, studies the piece of paper in her hand with total incomprehension. Out of the corner of her eye she takes in

George's mud-caked boots. Mrs Wetham is heard saying:

MRS WETHAM: Is it some sort of emblem?

George is patiently looking at her.

GEORGE: It's a skeleton, Mrs Wetham.

What she is looking at is a simple drawing of a skeleton with the words REMEMBER THINE END.

39

MRS WETHAM: But what's it for?

GEORGE: It's a design for a banner. For a Union.

MRS WETHAM: Union?

Mrs Wetham looks quite puzzled. George takes the cue to elaborate a little bit more.

GEORGE: A society of friends.

Mrs Wetham breaks into a relieved smile. Perhaps the word 'friends' has made it sound not so alarming after all. She chuckles engagingly.

MRS WETHAM: It's a most unusual request.

GEORGE: We'll pay a fair price.

Mrs Wetham has been perusing the paper again but looks up with her multiplication-table eyes.

MRS WETHAM: I'll speak with my husband.

With that she turns away towards the room at the back of the shop, closing the door behind her with a squeak.

George turns to consider the muddy trail his boots have made all the way from the entrance. Like a naughty schoolboy he makes a clean step aside as if to dissociate himself. At this moment we hear the door squeak open again, the same one that Mrs Wetham went through. George looks up stunned.

Mr Frampton is standing there sizing up George.

FRAMPTON: Mr Loveless. Good day.

George's face has lost a little of its composure. Somewhere in his mind his tiptoes are on the edge of a precipice.

FRAMPTON: Well, well, well. What brings you into town?

As he comes away the door behind him closes mysteriously.

Frampton takes a tour round the back of George.

FRAMPTON: I thought I detected Tolpiddle hereabouts.

On the word 'Tolpiddle' he carefully avoids the smears of wet mud. He has a print in his hand. He curves it away from him to indicate the environment.

FRAMPTON: So you are a lover of prints. Who would have guessed?

George doesn't turn to look at him.

GEORGE: I like to extend my mind whenever I can.

Frampton moves up alongside George, the print dangling behind his back, his height and build dwarfing his protagonist. He fetches up the print

confronting George with a Rowlandson amorous illustration. We can hear Frampton say:

FRAMPTON: How rewarding that one who uses his hands...

And see him continue:

FRAMPTON: Might also use his mind, Mr Loveless.

He walks away as George continues to look straight ahead.

GEORGE: An antidote to the sloth of countrifying, Mr Frampton.

We can hear Frampton snort, hear him rolling up the print. He is on the move again.

He considers the roll in his grasp. The image he may have in mind is that of a horse in heat.

FRAMPTON: The problem, Mr Loveless, is to match it, and having matched it, to use both hand and mind to exert it to some use. For a well-balanced appetite we must satisfy all our parts, eh Mr Loveless?

There is no reaction from George. Frampton is deflated.

FRAMPTON: Ah, but it's sad to see folk who are blind to their own interests.

GEORGE: Folk are not blind, sir, but it is those who master us that cannot see.

His hook is waiting to pin the fish.

FRAMPTON: Explain yourself, Loveless.

Frampton is quite taken aback by the sudden force of activity on George's part. We can hear George's footsteps.

When we next see him he is overlooking a print. His words when they come have a childlike innocence about them.

GEORGE: Here, for instance.

We see a view of the Nativity and in particular the head of the infant Christ.

GEORGE: Can you see this, sir?

A child's game, deserving of nothing better than a childish response, Frampton bows his head.

FRAMPTON: Yes.

There is a hint of cunning emerging in George's eye as he removes a solitary shilling from his purse.

His finger slides the coin across the paper to cover the infant face.

GEORGE: Can you see it now?

Frampton, with a great exertion of patience:

FRAMPTON: No.

GEORGE: What prevents you seeing it?

Frampton, with inexhaustible patience and boredom to match:

FRAMPTON: The silver, of course.

GEORGE: That's just it, sir.

The squeaking sound of the door opening at the back of the shop.

Mrs Wetham comes back inside.

Over by the main door Frampton is in a dark mood. He doffs his hat.

FRAMPTON: Mrs Wetham.

Mrs Wetham hurries to the door to open it.

MRS WETHAM: Mr Frampton.

With a last look as if smelling something rancid inside, he departs.

George is innocently studying prints through a zograscope.

MRS WETHAM: Mr Loveless, I'm afraid my husband is not at home.

It is one of the prints rather than the now frosty Mrs Wetham that occupies George's attention.

Mrs Wetham, in a fury fit to explode, holds the door wide open.

MRS WETHAM: He is away on business.

Suddenly Frampton reappears in the doorway.

FRAMPTON: Pass this through to your husband, Mrs Wetham . . .

A flustered Mrs Wetham finds herself in possession of the rolled-up print.

FRAMPTON: I almost forgot.

Then just as suddenly he is gone, and there is silence.

Mrs Wetham doesn't quite know what to do with herself or the object in her hand. She waves it about as if doing so would make it disappear. Her total awkwardness makes her giggle. She tries to dispense with it where it clearly won't go – well, it won't if one tries to treat something round as flat – and it bounces back at her.

So unflinching is George one would consider him to be making a special study of human folly.

With a little flick Mrs Wetham sends the offending roll atop a pile of rolls above her. All is fine until it seems the rolls have a mind of their own and before Mrs Wetham can say 'roll over', they do. Down they come, one after the other, and the more Mrs Wetham tries to control them the more they seem to be controlling her. What her hands can't manage, her upturned breasts abort quite nicely. And there she is with her human platform joined it seems forever to the piece of furniture before her. Mrs Wetham appears to be getting smaller but this could be because her knees are giving way. Now if she could only – her hand stretches out blindly and comes to rest on a trestle print stand – if she could use it to pull herself up, all might be well. Unfortunately the print stand also has a mind of its own and down it goes, taking Mrs Wetham, rolled prints and all. She flounders in the sea of paper.

As for George, he can't be a swimmer for he isn't jumping in to save her.

Mrs Wetham's face appears above the waves, gasping for air. In a frantic lunge for survival, she strikes out for land in the shape of a brass drawer handle. She grabs hold and hangs on tight. The whole drawer slides out to its full extent. A desperate Mrs Wetham, sensing the tidal wave about to descend on her, miraculously succeeds in sliding it back again. In an instinctive act of self-preservation, she reaches for the key and turns it. With a sigh of relief she anchors herself to her life-saver and, kicking back the waves with her dainty feet, up she comes.

Safe at last, she rests there momentarily to regain her battered composure. The framed picture on top of the cabinet of drawers wobbles uncertainly as just then the castors underneath come to life. Away it glides, and once more Mrs Wetham disappears from view, flying who knows where. The silence is broken as the picture crashes to the ground.

A dumbfounded Mr Wetham arrives upon the scene from his

little back room, just in time to find an unbalanced Mrs Wetham falling into his arms like a sack.

GEORGE: Mrs Wetham. Mr Wetham.

She and he look as if they are momentarily on ice.

At the door, George simply doffs an imaginary hat. There is a final shattering of something unseen as George leaves the shop.

Outside, we see the *trompe-l'oeil* picture once more, swaying to and fro in the Print Shop window.

George goes across the street in a jaunty frame of mind. The enclosed world of the Wethams' shop is not the whole world. Life is going on all about him, in the shape of a crocodile of Bluecoat schoolboys on an outing with their teacher; a tradesman with his bricks piled high upon his back; and a woman at an upstairs window putting out the bedclothes for an airing. Finally there is a man with a sandwich board and handbills, advertising DIORAMA, DORCHESTER FIELDS. POSITIVELY FOR ONE WEEK ONLY.

Mr Pitt, a gentleman in a top hat, comes out of the Courts. He appears to be looking for somebody. George comes hurrying up to meet him.

GEORGE: Mr Pitt.

PITT: George Loveless.

GEORGE: It's very kind of you to meet me, sir.

After shaking hands they move towards the brougham.

PITT: I thought we'd take a ride out of town.

GEORGE: Thank you, sir.

Mr Pitt taps the roof of the cab with his cane

and they are off. The hustle and bustle of Dorchester High Street is seen through the windows of the moving carriage.

The vehicle journeys in a curve through the countryside.

Mr Pitt and George are walking the windy summit of Maiden Castle, George more than usually animated.

The static vehicle with its driver more than a trifle bored.

Seen from afar, the two men take an endless circular walk in private and earnest conversation. Whatever their difference in social standing, they are equal on the massive earth.

Back in town, an exuberant George emerges out of an alley. Suddenly we hear gunshots

and see the Diorama Showman brandishing two pistols beside the 'stage door' of his entertainment. As he rushes back inside there is a clap of artificial thunder.

Through the 'stage door' we see the hypermanic activity of two stagehands, sharing sound and visual effects between them. They are opening and shutting flaps for light; sheet thunder is being intercut with lightning, then with rain; in turn they grab up violin and trumpet for musical effects; then one of them appears to have a moon on the end of a long stick, while the other one is struggling with a live cockerel.

George approaches the main entrance, not unlike the foyer to a cinema, and peers in.

Inside, a handful of people can be seen sitting before a vast screen depicting a village at night, a romantic view of reality. There is a drumroll and further distant noise of battle. Gradually the stars dissolve to dawn and there is the sound of the cock heralding the morning.

The Diorama Showman, a John Bull figure who talks more like P. T. Barnum, comes through and closes the door behind George and himself, shutting out the sights and sounds.

DIORAMA SHOWMAN: Did you want to buy a ticket to see the show?

He directs George's attention to a hoarding inviting him to DORCHESTER FIELDS – DIORAMA OF THE BATTLE OF WATERLOO. ADMISSION 6d. 3d.

GEORGE: There's none of us needs to bother with that. We'll be having a battle of our own soon enough . . . for nowt!

DIORAMA SHOWMAN: My dear sir, I think you underestimate the novelty of this unique and singular exhibition. The Diorama is the highest achievement of human skill and ingenuity – it cannot fail to give satisfaction – wonderfully instructive to youth and highly gratifying to mature age.

George is highly amused.

DIORMA SHOWMAN: My pictures represent the united labours of the finest artists and mechanicians. The weight of the costly apparatus is two tons. A change of view takes place

45

every other night, delineating the most interesting parts of the world in varying aspects of light and shade. Now, how about a trip to the other side of the world, tomorrow?

Over the old poster the Diorama Showman has pasted down a new hoarding proclaiming JOURNEY THROUGH THE ANTIPODES.

George reflects:

GEORGE: What you offer, sir, is illusion. It's the real world I'd like to see.

His voice sounds sad with longing and a touch of hopelessness:

GEORGE: In our short lives we move about so little, see so little.

His face brightens up, animates itself in such a way as to reach his companion with the fever of enthusiasm and hope.

GEORGE: Yes, I'd like to travel one day.

Off he goes, and we have the feeling that one day he will.

Young Stanfield and Brine are sprawled on the slope with nothing to do.

They are watching a small figure taking the curving road through the landscape.

George is passing along the lane. He stops for an 'aye'. Then having contemplated for a split second in time, he goes on his way putting up his hand in a farewell gesture.

Sounds of shooting. Two Gentleman Farmers are standing up in the open carriage with their shotguns pointing upwards.

George is standing by the hedge watching, as Brine and Young Stanfield catch up with him.

George is striding ahead. He looks small and frail but for all that there is something noble about him. He appears to be on his own. He stops a bit late, the way a dreamer might, and turns to see

Brine and Young Stanfield have fallen behind. The boys look a picture of rigid fascination.

The blonde-haired girl strokes her hair in a way that suggests she knows she is being studied. With her free hand she nudges the dark-haired girl, and they eye the boys flirtatiously.

George makes off, shaking his head in a good natured way.

Inside the carpenter's place, we see the green curtain has been put to a new use. George's skeleton is being beautifully rendered as a banner. We get a hint of the words REMEMBER THINE END as Bridget sews the cut-out letters on the tapestry. Her hand gathers the material closer across the table-top as she continues her stitching.

Her foot is rocking the baby's cradle.

John Hammett is busy carving what looks like a long pole. We see the deep concentration on his face.

His brother is sitting at the table, staring disconsolately at an empty plate. He glances round at a tired Bridget sitting at the other end of the bench. He takes hold of her hand to read her palm. She watches him, amused.

HAMMETT: You are going to have twenty-five children.

She laughs exasperation.

John sneaks a worried look at his own hand.

Bridget continues where she left off. She doesn't bother to look up.

BRIDGET: If you spent less time thinking about yourself and more time helping others . . .

Getting no response she looks up.

Hammett is imitating the solemn John as he works, and gets thumped by Bridget. She is suddenly quite serious.

BRIDGET: I mean it. For your own good.

She drags the excess material further on to the table.

BRIDGET: Getting on with the job never hurt anyone.

HAMMETT: Are you getting paid? Is he?

No answer.

HAMMETT: Only a fool does something for nothing.

Bridget rounds on him angrily.

BRIDGET: Those men paid a shilling out of their hard-earned money to join the Union. If you, and others like you, were to join . . .

Hammett slaps a coin on the table top. Bridget softens and moves the coin gently back towards him. She touches him affectionately.

BRIDGET: He believes in what he's doing.

HAMMETT: Don't worry about me . . .

He pockets the coin.

HAMMETT: I can look after myself.

At that Bridget rises quickly

causing the bench to unbalance. And down on his backside goes the independent Hammett.

Bridget pecks her husband on the cheek. She is clearly proud of him.

The hen is sniffing around aimlessly at the corner of a cottage. When the sound of cluck-cluck comes it takes no notice. Then a straw with its bushy head is there at the corner. It fidgets, pauses, fidgets again, then disappears out of sight tantalizingly. The hen follows, cackling softly. There is a sudden squawk.

Hammett makes off down the road with his shirt front bulging.

It is evening. John Hammett is standing outside the door to the upstairs room above the Stanfields' house. Behind him stand three blindfold figures. He knocks four times, and from within we hear James Loveless's voice.

JAMES: Who comes here to disturb the peace and harmony of this our most worthy and honourable order?

JOHN: I am a brother with strangers, who wish to be admitted into this your most worthy and honourable order.

We hear James repeat to those inside the room:

JAMES: Most worthy brothers, a brother stands at the door with strangers who wish to be admitted into this our most worthy and honourable order.

We hear a voice inside say, 'Let them enter.'

At the foot of the steps, Hammett is out in the dark keeping look-out. It is bitterly cold. He blows into his fingertips. There is the hint of the blonde-haired girl's hand and face before he

disappears from view. The sounds of a distant carriage passing
do not interrupt their intimacy.

Diana, Betsy, Sarah and Bridget, all the wives, are huddled
together in the Stanfields' room quietly applying themselves to
their work. Elvi joins them in sewing while Bridget is nursing
her baby. Charity has taken charge of Hetty. Now and then they
look to one another as if to reassure themselves. Somewhere
upstairs muffled voices are heard. Charity, although she appears
to be fully occupied, is well aware of what is happening. She
turns to watch the womenfolk, clearly putting everything
together in her own childlike way, her ear intent and her face
clouded with a sense of doom. Hetty distracts her with a tug,
back to their make-believe shadow play on the wall. Once again
we hear four distinctive knocks. Betsy raises her sad eyes to the
ceiling, and she whispers:

BETSY: Dear God, help them . . .

Inside the meeting room, the banner of the skeleton has been erected. The room, bathed in solitary oil light, is given an eerie look. The little space is crowded with twelve or fourteen men, sitting on benches sideways on, on either side. John Hammett and James Loveless have led three blindfold men to the centre where Old Stanfield is addressing them in their ritual.

> OLD STANFIELD: Strangers, within our secret walls we have admitted you;
> Hoping you will prove honest faithful just and true;
> If you cannot keep the secrets we require;
> Go hence you are at liberty to retire.

The three men remain still.

> OLD STANFIELD: Are your motives pure?
> MEN: Yes.

We see the assembly in the room, including Young Stanfield and Brine. The faces are dedicated.

> OLD STANFIELD: Then amongst us you will shortly be entitled to the endearing name of brother;
> And what you hear or see here done you must not disclose to any other;
> We are uniting to cultivate friendship as well as to protect our trade;
> And due respect must to all our laws be paid.
> Are your motives pure?

> MEN: Yes.

Those already initiated look satisfied.

Old Stanfield nods.

> JOHN: Give the strangers sight.

James Loveless removes the blindfold from one of the men's faces. His brow is sweaty as if he has come out of a nightmare. It is Legg.

Old Stanfield points to the skeleton.

> OLD STANFIELD: Strangers, mark well this shadow which you see;
> It is a faithful emblem of man's destiny.

George steps out of the darkness.

> GEORGE: Strangers, you are welcome and if you prove sincere;
> You'll not repent your pains and labour here;

We have one common interest and one common soul;
Which should by virtue guide and actuate the whole.

His recitation obviously has an emotional appeal to all those present.

GEORGE: The design of this our order is love and unity;
With self-protection founded on the laws of equity;
And when you have our mystic rites gone through;
Our secrets all will be disclosed to you.
We see a scroll tied with a red ribbon.

Now George takes Legg's right hand and leads him forward.

He places Legg's hand on a leather-bound volume, and in a gentle voice:

GEORGE: Edward Legg, do you swear to this alliance?

LEGG: I swear.

The face of the skeleton.

GEORGE: And now, shouldst thou ever prove deceitful, remember thine end. Remember.

Silence.

A crucified Christ dominating the altar. In his church, the Vicar is in the pulpit. He looks like one confronted with a problem.

VICAR: George. My dear friend. I like to consider myself a friend to all men. Indeed it's flattering of you to ask me to intervene, but . . .

George, lost in the pews, looks small by comparison, perhaps ashamed by his rashness in coming here.

VICAR: Don't you think you've got things a little out of proportion?

George looks cowed. He says almost to himself:

GEORGE: Difficult times, Vicar.

The Vicar separates his words more like a teacher to a pupil.

VICAR: Mr Frampton has not been ungenerous, as you can see . . .

The silver candelabra.

The altarpiece.

The stained-glass windows, now an explosion of colour against the sunlight, stand as a testament to Mr Frampton's generosity.

The Vicar and George stroll at leisure round the tree on the
village green, he with a friendly hand on George's shoulder.
Whatever George is saying to him he appears to nod approval.
He ends up shaking George's hand.

At the Big House, the Servant Girl opens an inner door.

SERVANT GIRL: Mr Frampton says would you please make
yourselves comfortable.

As they enter the room, George, James Loveless, Old Stanfield,
Young Stanfield, Brine and John Hammett are brought to a
halt. Across the room are the carpenter's six chairs.

The demure girl goes towards another door behind a screen. She
knocks politely and enters, closing it behind her. There is the
slightly muted sound of voices.

The flowers we can see are painted in an ornate frame above the
mantelpiece. But as we move, the three-directional picture
becomes that of a romantic ship at sea, and is finally
transformed into an idealized portrait of the laughing cavalier.
Is it one of Frampton's forebears – or perhaps another
metamorphosis of a more familiar figure?

James Loveless offers it the benefit of his fist.

They have all decided to remain standing, perhaps daunted by
the elaborate surroundings. There is a distant clink of glasses

and a guffaw from the next room. And still they wait. And still they stand.

Finally the door opens. Mr Frampton and the Vicar appear with the two Gentleman Farmers.

Mr Frampton, moving freely among the men, is courteous and friendly. He offers George his hand.

FRAMPTON: Good afternoon, gentlemen. George, I do hope we haven't kept you waiting. We had no idea of the time. Please accept my apologies.

He curves his hand towards the chairs.

FRAMPTON: Gentlemen, please . . . sit down.

Frampton, the Vicar and the Farmers assume their seats on one side of the green baize table, leaving the six Tolpuddle men to perch themselves stiffly on the carpenter's chairs some distance from the table.

One of the Farmers leans to speak in hushed tones with the Vicar. The Vicar answers him back and nods.

By the way George twists his feet we feel he senses he is being identified.

Frampton slaps his palm on the table.

FRAMPTON: Gentlemen. How good it is to see you all here. I think I can claim, in all modesty, to be a fair man . . .

There are nods from the two Gentlemen Farmers with a look that suggests he is being too modest already.

John Hammett has got to his feet, clutching a prepared statement.

JOHN: Mr Frampton, my friends asked me to come as an independent spokesman on their behalf . . .

Frampton cuts him short:

FRAMPTON: Yes, yes. I see no need to detain you any more than is necessary. The Vicar has put your case and we must admire his ability to see . . . both sides of the coin.

The Vicar looks quite smug.

Old Stanfield takes the piece of paper from John Hammett's hand and moves to the edge of the table.

OLD STANFIELD: We . . . we felt the time had come to put the . . .

Frampton reaches over and
screws the paper back into Old Stanfield's hand.

FRAMPTON: Of course you did, of course. And we have your best interests at heart...

JAMES: It's just that, well, we don't know where we are with the wages going down week by week...

FRAMPTON: You're quite right. There's no question of that.

Old Stanfield stands looking at his screwed-up piece of paper.

FRAMPTON: Despite the circumstances, and if I may add a fervent hope for the future, an extra shilling will be granted.

Pause.

GEORGE: Are you saying eight shillings?

FRAMPTON: Eight.

He clasps his hands together. The Vicar and the two Gentlemen Farmers concur.

FRAMPTON: Have you any questions, gentlemen?

But the men are too stunned to think of anything.

In the big kitchen, the Foreman is seated at table tucking into a huge plate of food, unconcerned that –

Nellie, the horse, is also standing there eating food from a plate similar to his own.

The Servant Girl has her hands on her hips like an old woman. She moves a stray bone on to an old copy of *The Times* and sorts out the rest of the joint. She places one or two good bits in her mouth and the remainder into the paper.

The Servant Girl skip-runs along the corridor running her hand along the bells and twirling the bundle like a play toy.

She opens the door and gives the bundle to someone on the outside.

SERVANT GIRL: Mr Frampton told me to give this to you.

We hear the sounds of profuse thank yous and see that it is Legg.

In front of Frampton's house, Legg goes away carrying his
bundle of food.

Legg's two children are there outside the barn on pay day. We
can hear the Foreman calling out the names and see the
labourers going on their way. One of them is Hammett. He
meets up with Brine, breathless from arriving late. Although we
can't make out what Hammett is saying, we can tell from his
gyrations all is not well inside the barn. At one moment he
opens his palm into which they both stare and the next he has
thrown the money down. Brine becomes as still as Hammett as
they stare at the offensive offering.

Inside the barn, the Clerk is at his place behind the desk.
   FOREMAN: Loveless.
The Clerk's hand slides across the table top. Whatever amount

it is we can only hear the coins grating where they lie hidden beneath the fingertips. The fingers withdraw to reveal six single coins. They remain there, their weight looking heavy for the waiting. Two neat rows of three.

The Clerk, who had expected trouble, relaxes as much as to say 'what could be easier'. His pen swivels into position, waiting. And above it all a friendly encouraging voice:

FOREMAN: Come on, George, one must eat to live.

George is standing nowhere near the desk. He looks at this moment more like a man philosophizing about his situation than an active body to it. He stands immovable among the other men. There is no sound to be heard. It is as if all hearts had stopped beating.

Then George is on his way. He goes leaving the doors ajar.

The Clerk and the Foreman gaze after him. There is silence.

Outside the barn George strides away and the remaining men follow him.

George storms into the church.

No sign of the Vicar.

George opens the vestry door. Still no sign of the Vicar.

The strikers spread out across the wasteland have the look of phantoms in a dark nightmare. They move quietly as they come to a grassy verge to look all in the same direction.

George is there, a harrowed face, watching

far beneath them, near the horizon, fires are silently burning. It is like another world, full of foreboding.

Next day the field is deserted.

Inside the gate stand Legg and two others. They lean on their forks, waiting, listening to the sound of approaching hoofs. As the horse carrying Frampton nears the gate the men move to meet him. Frampton leans down to shake their hands. After subdued smiles and a few inaudible pleasantries they move away. But Frampton detains Legg for some time.

The machinery is abandoned.

They are chock-a-block in the Stanfields' house, sharing with each other what little food they have, their spirits undaunted.

DIANA: Sing for us, Elvi.

Elvi is shy, feeling all eyes on her she covers her face.

YOUNG STANFIELD: Come on, Briney, we'll sing for them.

Brine and Young Stanfield break into song uninvited:

BRINE and YOUNG STANFIELD:
> When I was just a bardless boy
> No more than six years old
> I used to go a-keeping crows
> In rain and wind and cold . . .

Their sound leaves a great deal to be desired, as witnessed by John Hammett's pained expression

and James Loveless's laughter. Charity has her hands over her ears.

BRINE and YOUNG STANFIELD:
> And well do I remember now
> Ah well as it can be
> My little house, a hurdle thatched
> In the mash agin the sea
> Caa woo, caa woo,
> You old black crow
> Go fly away to Sutton
> If you stop here
> Twill cost you dear
> I'll kill you dead as mutton

There are a few cheers as they take a mock bow and collapse.

Elvi is in private confab with Sarah, and seems to have settled on something to sing.

Old Stanfield puts a finger to his mouth:

OLD STANFIELD: Ssssh!

Elvi sings her song all the while looking at her hands:

ELVI: It's fare thee well cold winter and fare thee well cold
> frost
> Nothing have I gained but my true love I've lost
> I'll sing and I'll be merry while a caution do I see
> And I'll rest me when I'm weary, let him go farewell
> he . . .

Brine watches looking a bit jealous. Elvi picks up his look and something about her penetrating gaze must tell him all he needs to know.

ELVI: To half a pound of reason take half a grain of sense
A small sprig of thyme and as much of prudence
And mix them up together as you may plainly see
I'll defy the lad forever, let him go farewell he.

When her song is ended there is silence.

Hetty, too young to know about life's hardness, laughs for the sake of laughing. Betsy, disturbed by the child, lifts her on to her lap, and glances across at –

George who is staring into space. He mutters:

GEORGE: Poor Legg.

A dead weasel caught in a trap.

In a copse, Hammett is in a crouching position, relieving himself. He glances away, first to one side then to the other, at the sound of knocking. He looks straight ahead at some distance through the trees and notices something of interest.

He gets up. Clutching his breeches about him, he hobbles forward and comes to examine a tree.

On the tree are a notice headed CAUTION and a WANTED notice for the Lanternist. There is a reward of twenty-five shillings. Hammett's hand snatches it off.

Meanwhile there is a lantern slide blazoning the wall. There are three soldiers standing in a row, all brightly coloured.

LANTERNIST: Who's the next one that we see in our galanty show?
Why it's three little soldier boys standing in a row...

The upstairs room has been turned into a makeshift theatre. The skeleton banner swung to one side has the appearance of a drape.

The Lanternist is in his element, entertaining the village children. He stands behind them rat-a-tat-tatting his fingers on a tambourine. By the wide-eyed look on the children's faces they are in the midst of battle.

LANTERNIST: Three little soldier boys, standing at the battle. They hear the horses gallop, they hear the sabres rattle.

Soon they'll wish that they were safely tucked up in their
   beds,
because 'bang' goes the cannon . . .

He pauses to get his timing right, relishing his moment of
suspense. In the ensuing silence he makes a sound like a rifle
retort, and with a flick of the wrist:

LANTERNIST: . . . and off comes their heads.

The soldiers are headless. This of course fetches yells of delight.

George sees the Lanternist up the dark hill.

At the top they hold hands.

LANTERNIST: I'm a changed man, George, a reformed one.
For you've swept the cobwebs out of my brain. I shall never
forget Tolpiddle.

George smiles.

GEORGE: Go then and make a Union of Lanternists.

We see them embrace.

The Lanternist walks into the open. We watch him consider the
sky, which as a man of his trade he is wont to do. With a gesture
of his hand, he turns and says:

LANTERNIST: See . . . the heavens!

George looks up

and sure enough there are the stars in all their infinite glory, so
bright and clear this night, they are a veritable lantern show
making the world of George and his companion seem small by
comparison. The Lanternist is heard calling a last farewell from
the distance.

George cups his hands to his mouth and calls:

GEORGE: Remember us. Remember.

And the sound echoes across the empty landscape.

A fist bangs on the door.

They are lying three abed – George, Betsy and Hetty – in the
darkened room. George turns out of his sleep. He has the look
of one unsure of anything. The knock comes again.

There is a Constable standing outside the door.

Slowly George descends the stairs.

The Constable paces up and down.

George moves towards the door. Having opened it he stands there stunned.

CONSTABLE: George Loveless?

George doesn't answer.

CONSTABLE: George Loveless?

There is a deep finality in George's sigh.

GEORGE: Yes.

We study the WARRANT FOR ARREST.

Beyond his captor, Old Stanfield and Young Stanfield are standing in the road waiting. They are linked by a chain. A few feet away stands Brine. A little further than that, yet somehow closer as if he desperately needed to keep contact, is James Loveless. Finally the face of Hammett. Hammett?

George looks as though he were seeing things.

Hammett already has his finger to his lips, moving it gently from side to side. Having registered contact he drops his hand.

George is handcuffed

and led away with the others by the Constable on horseback.

Whatever secrets the Union House kept within its walls have evaporated. Now there is only the sound of the horse and the men marching. It is as if they will never come back to this place;

or to the tree on the village green, drifting away;

or to the landscape so familiar to them, this landscape that even now stretches forth in an explosion of light, rich but oblivious.

It is the same light, though very subdued, that fills the open doorway to a cell. In a moment one of the men is thrust inside, then the door runs home with a thud shutting darkness inside. We hear the sound of five other doors closing one by one, each descending in volume as it moves further away. Then out of the ensuing silence, four distant but distinctive taps, repeated six times one after the other. They grow in volume, conveying the men's resistance.

The crown of England tapestried into a canopy.

Mr Frampton stands in the court room. Around him the place seems empty. We hear the cultivated voice of Mr Pitt:

PITT: These labourers . . .

Frampton looks sour.

Mr Pitt is standing in the dock.

PITT: . . . I use the word with the utmost respect, are worthy and honourable men. I have met George Loveless on several occasions. He is an honest man. He told me the men work hard.

Frampton studies his hand for dust and flicks his finger tips to remove any.

PITT: These men have a right to a decent wage for a decent job well done. Beyond this county the wage of half a pound is tolerated.

Frampton demurs.

PITT: The solution is simple. A magistrate should fix the sum by law as has always been the custom.

FRAMPTON: I am a magistrate, Chairman of the Bench and a member of the Grand Jury.

Mr Pitt is unperturbed and turns to look up at the balcony.

PITT: Vicar, I understand you were an advocate for the Tolpiddle men . . .

The Vicar leans forward, looking as awkward as one in the middle of a see-saw.

PITT: And that you were present when Mr Frampton agreed to rectify their grievances.

The Vicar glances in the direction of one then the other. He nods.

PITT: Were they not promised an extra shilling?

Frampton's face grows dark with foreboding.

PITT: Well?

The Vicar, toying with his crucifix, coughs as if clearing a dry throat.

The court's tabby cat is poised waiting for a mouse.

63

The whole place seems to be waiting.

VICAR: No . . . no such promise was made.

PITT: Are you quite certain?

FRAMPTON: He is a man of God.

Mr Frampton sounds outraged. He picks up his hat and cane as if to dismiss further discussion. Then he turns back in a last attempt to reason:

FRAMPTON: Please don't make a fool of yourself, Mr Pitt. The men's wages are neither here nor there. But they were engaged in secret meetings, administering illegal oaths, taking the law into their own hands. That must stop.

He is warming to his theme:

FRAMPTON: See what happened in France! Do you want this country awash with blood? Our blood.

Up in the gallery the Vicar is and clearly has been taking consolation in his flask of brandy.

Mr Pitt attempts to bring things back to earth.

PITT: We are talking about a Union of farm labourers which may be offensive to some but is no longer against the law. All this nonsense about 'illegal oaths', it's a trumped-up charge.

Frampton sounds indignant:

FRAMPTON: It's on the Statute Book.

Mr Pitt is reluctantly forced to concede.

The Vicar is disappearing quietly out the door, as Frampton's tone becomes more placatory.

FRAMPTON: Mr Pitt, you're a magistrate. I can tell you, in the strictest confidence . . .

The Vicar pricks up his ears and comes back to listen.

FRAMPTON: I have it from no less a person than the Home Secr . . . on the very highest authority – this is the best way to proceed. We have followed every letter of the law.

He enumerates on the fingers of one hand.

FRAMPTON: Cautions were posted . . .

PITT: Yes, two days before their arrest on an offence alleged as many months before.

Frampton carries on regardless:

FRAMPTON: The men were charged before Charles Wollaston...

PITT: Your brother!

VICAR: Half-brother, actually.

Emboldened by brandy, the Vicar has suddenly become a stickler for accuracy.

Frampton still carries on regardless.

FRAMPTON: William Ponsonby committed them for trial at the Assizes...

PITT: The Home Secretary's brother!

The Vicar leans over the balcony, grown bolder still.

VICAR: Brother-in-law, actually.

Frampton is determined not to be distracted.

FRAMPTON: And Judge Williams will hear the case in this very court.

Mr Pitt is alarmed.

PITT: Judge Williams?

He looks pointedly in the direction of the Vicar.

PITT: Herod's brother!

The Vicar is lost for words and in his confusion accidentally knocks his hat off the edge of the balcony. Casting his eye downwards, he looks as if he is seeing things.

His hat seems to be taking a walk on its own.

Ignoring this interruption, Mr Pitt makes a sweeping gesture and points to the canopy. We follow the direction of his finger.

PITT: Yes, and the King's brother, he also administers 'illegal oaths' as Grand Master of the Orange Lodge. One law for the rich, another for the poor.

The Vicar is making an unsteady exit along the courtroom corridor. The court tabby pursues him.

PITT: The whole thing is a monstrous game, a political box-of-tricks, with the cards stacked against innocent men. But there's one card left to be played. Public opinion.

Frampton has had enough. He makes to walk away and practically throws his last few words over his shoulder.

FRAMPTON: You would be well advised to forget George

Loveless and his kind. No one wants to know them. And no one will remember them.

We descend to the bowels of the building, where the cells seem like hell's abode.

In the courtroom corridor, children are getting crushed in the throng as the public are trying to squeeze themselves through the courtroom door. Arms and legs are jammed as an Usher struggles to get the door shut.

USHER: I'm terribly sorry but the court is full.

A bar drops into position securing the way in.

Frosted glass obscures a clear view into the courtroom. Somewhere among abstract shapes we can hear words that seem to come from another planet. The accused are being called. They ascend from the depths, taking shape as they emerge to the surface only to be lost again in the general hubbub of officialdom.

The corridor has emptied except for the wives and children of the men. Unable to fight their way in, they huddle together, a picture of unrelenting despair.

Mrs Brine stares at the shadowy gestures as if trying to read them. The same goes for Sarah and Diana, for Elvi and for the blonde- and dark-haired girlfriends.

Bridget Hammett looks as if she is involved in a private agony to herself. She clutches her baby in a haphazard way as if she held the child to blame. Sarah relieves her of the child.

She clutches it to her, warming its face against her responsible breast.

Through the frosted glass an occasional shadow gives rise to the drama emanating from within.

Betsy turns, hearing approaching footsteps.

They continue to be heard where the corridor takes a turning. Gradually the figures emerge into the corridor itself. The Constable who arrested the men is carrying a scroll tied with a red ribbon. The two Gentlemen Farmers. And there is just the elbow of another man where he has placed his fist on his waist. All of them have stopped as if waiting for directions.

Betsy cranes her neck a little bit more.

The figure with the protruding elbow is Edward Legg.

More footsteps as Mrs Wetham from the Print Shop emerges, looking a little lost in awe of her surroundings. Conscious of the eyes on her, she fusses with her dress.

She is carrying George's sketch of the skeleton.

Just then the Usher comes, all hands fluffing, making calm and apology and hurry. He makes a circle with his finger suggesting the witnesses have to go round to the other side of the courtroom. Like a gentleman bred, he extends his hand for them to go back the way they have come. He goes with them, leaving a momentary emptiness behind.

Behind the glass, distorted shapes appear to be rising in a wave of fury.

Two pigeons fluttering wildly in their basket.
Diana is holding on to Charity back at the Stanfields' house. Behind them John Hammett's voice is talking continuously in the manner of dictating a letter. As if from another room there is the sound of Betsy wailing like a hurt dog. Now and again Charity picks out a word from the dictation.

    CHARITY: What does tran... transp...

    DIANA: Transportation.

    CHARITY: ... mean?

    DIANA: It means they're going a long way away on a boat.

    CHARITY: Seven years is a long time.

Diana says nothing.

    DIANA: I'm seven, aren't I?

Diana tightens her grip instead of replying.

Legg progresses down the village street. He looks a pale shadow of his former self. His way is clear until two labourers appear going towards him. However after a few yards the labourers cross the road on a slant. Now they are walking in parallel but opposite to Legg. After a few yards the labourers cross the road again once more on a slant. They continue on their way with their backs to Legg. Finally Legg turns round, sensitive to their detour.

Legg bangs the knocker on the door of Frampton's house. He

waits. The place is country quiet except for the growling of a dog. The Servant Girl hardly opens the door.

SERVANT GIRL: Mr Frampton is not at home. He is away on business.

LEGG: When will he be back?

The Servant Girl seems a bit lost here. She glances back inside the house, screwing up her face as if she was trying to understand something inside.

Legg looks crestfallen. He hears her answer:

SERVANT GIRL: I don't know.

She shares Legg's gloom for a moment before closing the door on him.

Through the window, we watch Legg walk away. When he turns we can see, in his own simpleton way, he knows.

Across the room we see Frampton, Wollaston and the two Gentlemen Farmers where they sit at the gaming table with decanter and glasses.

GENTLEMAN 1: Seven years out of mischief...

He looks flushed from the wine and the warmth of the room.

GENTLEMAN 1: I think them jolly lucky.

He punctuates the last word with a slap of the card going down.

GENTLEMAN 1: How I would love to visit Botany Bay. Have you read Cook?

His enthusiasm doesn't work on Frampton, who looks distracted.

GENTLEMAN 2: Reading is for the leisured class.

Gentleman 1 roars at that.

GENTLEMAN 2: When it falls into the wrong hands...

He proffers his card in a sneaky way.

GENTLEMAN 2: It is a corrupter of morals.

Wollaston nods soberly.

WOLLASTON: Strange chance that rabble-rouser Loveless falling ill, what?

While waiting for his turn to play, with his free hand he idly flicks the unused pack of cards lying face down on the table beside Gentleman 2. He looks closer, his curiosity aroused.

We see that the spare pack has been marked with a pencil dot along the edge of each card so that in animation it appears to roll to and fro.

GENTLEMAN 1: Can't exercise his evil powers over those gullible friends of his any more.

GENTLEMAN 2: Now we can keep an eye on him, at least until he gets to Plymouth.

He carefully moves the offending pack away from Wollaston to his other side.

GENTLEMAN 2: Next thing we know the wives will be asking for Parish Relief.

GENTLEMAN 1: No family is entitled to Relief who can afford to pay a shilling to join a Union.

He lays down several pounds for his bet.

GENTLEMAN 2: Their leaders are simply feathering their own nests.

WOLLASTON: I wonder if he really is the ringleader or whether there aren't others, what? Some shadow puppet-master up in London manipulating him with rods.

Frampton jerks awkwardly as though he is the one who has been manipulated.

GENTLEMAN 1: It's a conspiracy, I'll wager.

WOLLASTON: I went to see him in his cell the other day, and offered to intercede on his behalf if he would name the names. He struck the same truculent attitude as the day my brother had him brought before me on the bench . . .

He is holding his cards rather carelessly.

WOLLASTON: 'No, Mr Wollaston,' says he, 'I would rather undergo any punishment than betray my fellow members.'

GENTLEMAN 2: All self-righteous innocence, eh?

As he speaks he eyes his neighbour's hand.

WOLLASTON: I told him, 'Loveless, I am sorry to see a man like you in such a situation, but it is your own fault, you are a wicked stubborn fellow who wanted a breaking . . .'

GENTLEMAN 1: And we saw that he got it.

WOLLASTON: D'you know what he said? He asked me if I was in my right mind. 'Ah,' said I, 'it's no use talking to you, what?' 'No, sir,' said he, 'not unless you talk more reasonable.'

Frampton still appears to be someplace else. Gentleman 1 glances at Gentleman 2 as much as to say, 'We are playing a game of cards, aren't we?' Gentleman 2 looks as though he is doing some quick mental work.

FRAMPTON: In some strange way I can't help admiring him. I can't put my finger on it exactly. Even when all was lost, he had the uncanniest look in his eye as if somehow he had won.

His voice trails away. By the look on his face we get the feeling George will haunt his conscience like a ball coming back to float on top of the water.

Gentleman 1 sneaks a distasteful look in the direction of Gentleman 2. Wollaston puts out his last card. Gentleman 1 quickly tops it, looking at Frampton as much as to say, 'You should keep your mind on the game.' Frampton throws in his card. But then Gentleman 1 closes his eyes as if the sun had agonized him when Gentleman 2 plays the winning card.

Gentleman 2 takes the spoils, a display of amazing wealth.

Frampton puts the top on the decanter and we hear him rise.

He strides across the room. Reaching the door, he doesn't bother to turn.

FRAMPTON: Good night, gentlemen.

Frampton goes out leaving the doors open behind him.

He climbs the dark stairs, a black figure in his soul and in history.

Legg hoists up his rickety furnishings into the wagon. There isn't much but he protects them with the straw as if they were precious to him.

He goes inside the house. There is a broken window. He stands inside looking at this place where he has probably lived the best part of his life.

Sound of the door banging, reverberating. Legg is pulling the wagon away. One of his two little girls turns her head among the rubble of belongings to look at him. Such an old face for so young a child.

Mrs Brine is standing at her door, arms folded. As the sound comes near she steps quickly into the road.

She waves the vehicle to a halt. The wagon stops before her. Ignoring Legg she goes out of sight behind the vehicle.

Mrs Brine envelops Legg's two small children with her shawl

and crosses the remainder of it over their fronts tucking them in.

Legg turns to watch. The woman's simple act intensifies the guilt he feels inside him.

Joseph peers round the door.

The wagon trundles away taking its two pathetic little faces. One of them manages a wave as if she were for all the world going on a holiday.

Joseph returns the wave, while Mrs Brine stands there sharing their desperation.

The wagon turns a corner and disappears, leaving a void.

A crackling sound and flickering firelight. In the corner, Hetty is frightened from an acute sense of something out of odds. Sound of the door latch. The child looks round.

The door is bolted. Now there is a gentle knock.

SARAH: Betsy. Hetty.

Betsy is sitting by the fireside. She doesn't react to the knock when it comes again or to the footsteps moving away. There is a leather-bound book dangling from her hand. She peruses it, her face showing the barest hint of a smile.

Inside the book, we read in an honest scroll, GEORGE LOVELESS 1830. Sound of the page turning. Having turned it reads in bold print PHILOSOPHY.

Betsy throws the book into the fire.

Hetty is accumulating any other books she can find. Perhaps understanding this need, she fetches them and places them in her mother's lap with a deep sigh of exhaustion. Betsy shows no reaction.

HETTY: Bad books.

We hear Betsy laugh, see her clutching the child to her. When Betsy can find words they come in a whisper in the child's ear:

BETSY: It's not the books that's bad, my cherub.

Her voice breaks. She shushes the child in a way that is really nursing herself.

Next day, the books, what can be rescued of them, are sifted from the ashes by a dumbfounded Sarah.

73

In the early hours of morning, a horseman leads five of the men, Old Stanfield and Young Stanfield, Brine, Hammett and James Loveless. They are moving best they can along the path between the fields neath the weight of the clanking chains that bind them together.

The Constable on his horse leads them through the village's deserted street. A solitary lamp shining like a beacon, twisting and turning in the breeze, is the only evidence of life in this otherwise ghostly place.

In the quietness of dark rooms their families lie asleep in bed. All except Elvi who opens her eyes as the sound of distant clanking reaches her.

Pulling a shawl about her she comes outside.

But there is nothing to be seen. Just a rhythmic sound dying to nothing.

A message is tied to a pigeon's leg.

Charity is looking in wonderment at the pigeon in her hands. Standing outside the house beside her, John Hammett smiles. There is a flutter of wings

as the pigeon takes to the skies. Away, away it goes until it all but disappears.

The horses' hoofs and the wheels of the stagecoach take the corner.

They stampede down the middle of the village street. The place is quite deserted, as if the people are still in mourning or have no heart for the open air. The stagecoach passes through the village without stopping and disappears behind a hedge, where if it wasn't for the coachmen sitting on top it would be almost invisible.

The vehicle stands in a shady spot outside the village. Printed in gold across the side is LONDON – DORCHESTER. There is something unnerving about the silence.

Then Charity and Joseph come running towards it.

The dark-haired girl brings tankards on a tray. She intercepts a signal from the blonde-haired girl, who runs off in the opposite direction.

The two liveried coachmen down their liquid refreshment.

Charity and Joseph are frozen with curiosity. Then Joseph tentatively steps forward while Charity holds back.

A Ranger is sitting benignly at the open window. He shushes them and indicates that the other passengers are asleep. He takes a thaumatrope out of his pocket and prepares to twirl it for the benefit of the children. On one side the disc shows a bird and on the other side an empty cage.

As it spins we see the bird inside the cage.

Joseph and Charity are fascinated. At the sound of distant running, the Ranger tucks the disc in Joseph's top pocket with his finger and Joseph smiles victoriously.

Suddenly John Hammett runs up out of breath –

to receive a leather satchel from the Ranger. Nothing is said.

But on his way, as the stagecoach takes the corner, the Ranger puts his arm out of the window with its fist firmly clenched against the breeze.

Inside the Stanfields' house, two hands empty the contents of the satchel across the table top, hinting at something sparkling. On the wooden surface lies a pile of shilling coins.

The women sit there looking at the table. In their eyes a look of sadness and awe. Betsy looks at Diana then back at the table. Sarah watches.

John Hammett looks as pleased as Punch. In contrast to the haunted-looking women he looks as though he has made up his mind to cope in the other men's absence. He peruses documents in a matter-of-fact way.

 BETSY: Where's it coming from?

John puts a finger to his mouth.

 BETSY: I don't want anything that doesn't belong to me. I couldn't touch it.

 SARAH: Trust him, Betsy.

But Betsy looks as though she doesn't know the word any more. Diana embraces her in a way that makes them both look strong.

 JOHN: It won't make up for what's happened, but it'll help. It comes from London. People from all walks of life are taking up our cause, calling themselves the London–

Dorchester Committee. They've started a petition. . .
meetings are being called all over the country. . . questions in
Parliament. They're asking me to see that you and the
children don't go wanting. They want you to have it. It's a
gift. And it will come every week.

A moment's silence.

DIANA: The Lord be praised.

Betsy hurries out the door.

She runs across the street, calling excitedly:

BETSY: Hetty. Hetty.

The child comes running to the mother who, taking her up in
her arms, swings her joyfully round. Hetty has never seen a face
so radiant.

BETSY: People are good.

Betsy clutches the child to her in gratitude.

Diana stands in the gloom of the upstairs room.

Ahead of her are the two rows of pews, and beyond that the
banner of the skeleton proclaiming its motto REMEMBER THINE
END.

After a moment she rolls up her sleeves with grim determination
and moves forward.

She opens the window and floods the place with light.

With one tug she pulls down the banner.

In next to no time, Elvi and Charity are briskly sweeping the
floor, and

the room has been rearranged with the forms in a square as for a
meeting. Diana stands directing activity as Sarah and Bridget
are hanging a new trailer proclaiming LONDON – DORCHESTER
COMMITTEE.

A Gaoler turns the key and opens the cell door.

GAOLER: Are you up to walking, sir?

George, looking pale and weak, looks up.

GEORGE: I'm not likely to outdo you.

GAOLER: We're having to pass through the town. Let me
remove them.

77

George glances down.

His feet are bound in chains.

George gives him a sympathetic look and smiles.

   GEORGE: It's all right. I'm not ashamed.

George shuffles out of his cell and along the passage. He is
followed by the Gaoler who hangs his keys on a hook as he
passes.

Reaching the courtyard George's words rampage the silence. In his mind's eye he can see the ghostly faces of his departed comrades.

GEORGE: We have injured no man's reputation, character, person or property. We were uniting together to preserve ourselves, our wives and our children from utter degradation and starvation.

The Gaoler stands at the main door. There is no doubt that the shame lies with him.

His hands descend to the massive bolt and he draws it back with a resounding clack. We hear the hectic sounds of the street.

George's constrained feet trudging down Dorchester High Street, closely followed by the Gaoler's boots.

A distant glimpse of Mrs Wetham at her Print Shop door. Having seen all she wants to see, she closes it and pulls down the blind.

At times a solitary glimpse of town feet, at others a crowd of either nondescript or bare feet.

Across the street a group of labourers digging a hole. They stop work to watch, their faces peeping up above ground level. One of them crosses himself.

We become aware of George fidgeting with something inside his sleeve. A piece of paper falls to the ground.

George's feet and rumbling carriage wheels seen beyond railings.

An old Tramp watches from where he is hunched up on the basement steps. The events have a fascination for him,

His eyes widen in amazement,

particularly since the passing carriage wheels, when seen through the vertical slats of the railings, create an odd optical illusion. It is as if time has stopped the wheels in the process of turning and is pulling the spokes back in a weightless curve.

The Tramp closes his eyes. When he opens them again

there is just the crumpled piece of paper lying there in the roadway.

His hand retrieves the paper.

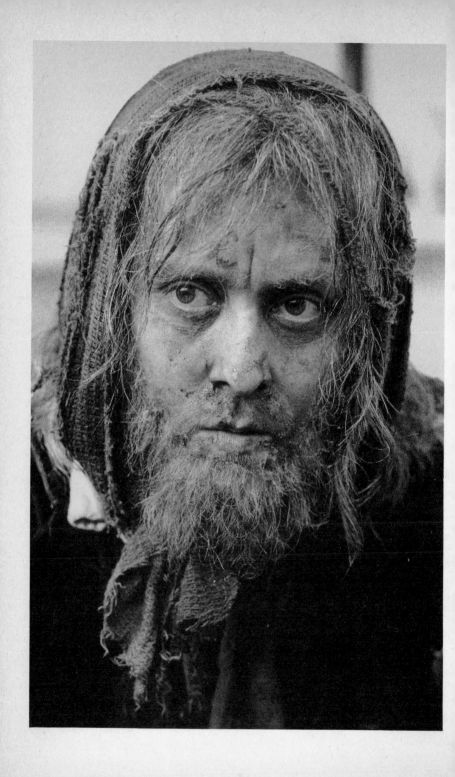

He hobbles across the street, continuing to look at the ground as though he hopes to find something more. He hands the paper to a gentleman bystander, pointing down to where he made his find.

The possessor of the paper is Mr Pitt. He looks up, turns.

We can see George now some distance away going up the street.

Mr Pitt reads from the paper:

PITT: 'God is our guide! From field, from wave,
From plough, from anvil and from loom,
We come, our country's rights to save,
And speak the tyrant faction's doom;
We raise the watchword "Liberty",
We will, we will, we will be free!'

George has reached the end of the road where there is an exchange of papers and a carriage waiting. He is helped on to the carriage.

PITT: 'God is our guide! No swords we draw,
We kindle not war's battle fires,
By reason, union, justice, law,
We claim the birthright of our sires;
We raise the watchword "Liberty",
We will, we will, we will be free!'

The vehicle has turned amid the clatter of hoofs, comes towards us for a bit. Among the sightseers children run alongside. The carriage turns a corner disappearing from sight.

Mr Pitt is still looking after it has gone.

PITT: He meant this for you and others like you, not for me.

He hands the paper back to the Tramp, who looks moved as if he had never been given anything before.

PITT: When you have done with it, don't throw it away. Let it go from hand to hand. My task will be to teach the members of my class, injustice cannot be allowed to go unchallenged.

With that he hurries away, a sense of determination in his stride. The town is alive with a clatter of hoofs and wheels.

Betsy takes the country road, the same one George had taken. On the slope sit the blonde-haired and dark-haired girlfriends in place of Brine and Young Stanfield. Betsy stops briefly to say 'aye' just as George had done. And the two girls reply likewise. Then some way past, Betsy puts up her hand in a farewell gesture that is uncannily like George.

The ship on a calm sea in Plymouth harbour.

George takes the steep dangling rope ladder, his body rising up like an ascension.

Over the slat. It slides open. George descends, disappearing from view.

Another slat opening. Dark. Again George descending from view.

Yet another slat. Darker. Yet again George descending from view.

We see the words others have left behind, names, dates, places, vows, scratched into the wood that comprises the walls of the lowest deck. Finally there is the seeping through the floor of the flotsam and jetsam. The silence is broken intermittently by the dungeon sound of water hitting like a skull compressed.

A seagull's call. Betsy is sitting on the sea wall clutching a letter. Sound of water lapping the shingle, sucking back, lapping again. The water seems to hold a fascination for her.

The ship has gone. We hear George Loveless speak his letter to his wife.

> GEORGE: I thank you, my dear wife, for the kind attention you have ever paid me, and you may safely rely on it that as long as I live it will be my constant endeavour to return that kindness in every possible way, and that I shall never forget the promise made at the Altar; and though we may part awhile, I shall consider myself under the same obligations as though living in your immediate presence. Be satisfied, my dear, on my account. Depend upon it, it will work together for good and we shall yet rejoice together. I shall do well for He who is the Lord of the wind and waves will be my support in life and death.

An endless drifting silent sea.

An eerie sound of a roller turning. George's journey is told by way of a painted panorama. This is how an artist in George's day might see it for the enlightenment of children. We have only to turn the roller to unfold the world.

The British Channel
    Brittany
        Bay of Biscay
            Cape St Vincent
                Tenerife
                    Cape Verde
                        Sierra Leone
                            South Atlantic Ocean
                          Equator
                              Ascension Island
                            St Helena
                                Cape of Good Hope
                                Indian Ocean
                                  Cape Leeuwin

The moving panorama has turned until it stops at Australia. We can see Van Diemen's Land and Botany Bay.

A squawk of gulls. The Captain has displayed the toy panorama for the benefit of a Foppish Gentleman.

CAPTAIN: For just one penny you can put the world in your pocket.

FOP: Absolutely charming toy.

They are sitting at the helm of a rowboat coming ashore from the convict ship with a party of boy convicts.

FOP: Nice journey, Captain?

CAPTAIN: Profitable. At a pound a head it pays to keep the scum alive.

The Fop examines the toy as curious as a child. He holds the panorama up to the light.

FOP: British?

CAPTAIN: Only the very best, my dear sir.

The Fop decides to make a purchase and searches in his purse to find the requisite coin.

FOP: Done!

The Fop grins. He slaps his money in the Captain's outstretched palm.

A boy, barely a youth, one of the complement in the boat, turns, hearing music coming from the shore.

From the topmost mast a fluttering Union Jack flapping victoriously free.

Below the mast is a lone Aborigine. He looks like a mascot in his naval-officer coat and hat. He is dancing a pathetic version of the sailor's hornpipe to the accompaniment of a tin whistle and clapping hands.

The remainer of his kind – there are a bundle of them – look the worse for drink. One of the sailors comes to pour a flask down one of their throats.

The sailors' inane laughing faces.

A pair of manacles are removed from feet and relegated to the pile.

The convicts form a snake line towards the tables.

On to the table top is placed a cloth and into this is dumped a collection of foodstuffs. The whole is knotted. This in turn is pushed along towards hands stuffing a blanket into a pack. The pack is finally dispensed to the other side of the table.

REGISTRAR: Name?

GEORGE: Loveless.

A paper is offered up. George takes it.

REGISTRAR: Next.

The hand makes a waving-away gesture.

GEORGE: Where do I go?

REGISTRAR: It's all there.

George looks totally lost, even fretful.

GEORGE: Yes, but . . . where is it?

REGISTRAR: That's for you to find out. Next.

George finds himself forced to the side to make room for the next man.

Then he is standing by the wayside for all the world like a lost waif, until the Registrar's hand snatches the paper from him.

REGISTRAR: It's about three hundred miles. Should take you nine days, strong fellow like you. Don't eat your rations all at once or you'll starve.

The hand points.

REGISTRAR: That way.

A country road. George comes with a pack on his back, but trudging as if he were still mentally in chains. He stops to consider

the landscape. A dense forest that seems to swamp the mountains all the way to the horizon. Out of the silence we can hear a small pathetic voice.

CHARLIE: Mister.

The boy from the boat is standing where two paths diverge.

CHARLIE: Could you help me?

He looks desperately pleading.

CHARLIE: I don't know which way to go.

The boy holds out the paper he was given.

George looks at the boy for a long time. Perhaps he is thinking of the children he knew back in the village. He smiles broadly.

George and Charlie are eating by the wayside. George has his pack open on his lap. The boy proceeds to reach for his own. George hands him some food.

GEORGE: Take it.

The boy eats, all the time looking at George as if he was unreal. George tucks his food supply away in his bag.

CHARLIE: Look.

The boy puts out his hand to George showing his palm branded with the letter C.

CHARLIE: C stands for convict.

George shows his own hand also branded with the letter C, then takes hold of the boy's hand.

GEORGE: No, comrades.

George kisses the boy's hand.

GEORGE: What's your name?

85

CHARLIE: Charlie.

GEORGE: Well, there you are, you see. Things are more than they appear.

He lets Charlie's hand go.

CHARLIE: What's yours?

George thinks for a moment.

GEORGE: Christopher.

The boy smiles.

CHARLIE: No, it isn't.

George laughs. The boy nibbles the remains of something. They are together yet separate, each in his own private world.

A short way away in the deep grass there is a colourful bird.

CHARLIE: Men are bad.

George considers his young companion.

GEORGE: Are you bad?

The boy gives George a double take, smiles broadly and shakes his head.

GEORGE: So not all men are bad.

The boy gives him a brief glance as much as to say, 'I suppose so.'

GEORGE: The truth is that men are born good.

Charlie nods unconvinced. Something in George won't let the subject pass without making his point.

GEORGE: Tell me. If we planted apples in this field and the fruit grew rich and strong, and we planted apples in that field and the fruit didn't grow rich and strong, what's to blame?

CHARLIE: Mmm?

GEORGE: Go on.

CHARLIE: The apples what didn't come out right, of course.

GEORGE: No. We could have planted them here and they'd have been all right.

The boy shrugs.

CHARLIE: Some of them would have come out all right anyway.

George nods.

GEORGE: True. Some would survive in spite of everything. But we want them all to grow, don't we?

The boy looks at him reflectively.

CHARLIE: You sound like a preacher.

GEORGE: I'm sorry. I didn't mean to.

CHARLIE: It's all right, you don't look like one.

George looks as pleased as a king in disguise. Suddenly we hear a whipcrack
then catch sight of a horse and rider on the road.

GEORGE: Wait there, don't move. You might be in luck here.

He hurries up the slope.

GEORGE: Whoa, whoa there.

Left alone for a moment or two, Charlie sneaks George's food out of his pack and into his own. Meanwhile we can hear George trying to persuade the traveller to help.

GEORGE: He's got some papers. It's got a place name on it, but I don't know because I'm new round here myself. I wonder if you could help him or if you know where that is?

Then we see George urgently beckon the boy to approach while the rider considers the lad's papers.

GEORGE: Charlie, up here, quick.

When he comes, there is an astonished look on Charlie's face as if in his wildest dreams he had never seen such a sight.

We are surprised to see the face of a beautiful woman dressed in man's clothing. She breaks into a smile.

MRS CARLYLE: Right, get him up.

GEORGE: Come on, Charlie, quickly. You're in luck, lad.

George hoists him up behind the rider.

GEORGE: Hold on.

MRS CARLYLE: Fetch his pack then.

George comes with a pack and puts it round the boy's shoulders.

GEORGE: Thank you, mam. Bless you, boy.

As they ride away, George goes about getting his own things together.

At some point along the way the boy turns, a vexed face.

George is nowhere to be seen.

Pack on his back, George has taken to the forest.

A peaceful lakeside. George has found himself an idyllic spot, sitting on the bank. He removes his pack. He bares his feet, letting them hover above the water as if savouring the luxury to come. He smiles inwardly to himself at the thought of it. He touches the water.

His eyes are closed. He is as still as if his heart had stopped. The expression is distilled ecstasy and pain. He draws his feet up, causing the water to gulp, and down again crashing it.

He takes his pack on to his lap. He pauses a moment.

GEORGE: For what we are about to receive may the Lord make us truly thankful. Amen.

He opens his pack. He looks in. Looks taken aback. George takes out not one supply of food but two, which gives him some food for thought.

Endless chains of mountains collide with one another creating a valley for the forest. The trees appear about to overtake everything. While George never doubted the beauty in human life, the earth he had known in his homeland was merely a back-breaking place. Now he is in paradise and something comes to him, nudges the inside of him, of all that is magnificent at the hand of his God. Now and then he stops to hear the birds sing and they seem to be singing for him. In some strange way he is captive yet free and his heart is full.

At the top of the mountain he can see the world as God made it. No one can answer him back here. He can even voice his opinions and they will come back to him treblefold. He puts his hands to his mouth and shouts at the top of his lungs

GEORGE: We will...

And the echo carries over the landscape:

We will, we will...

GEORGE: ...be free...

...be free, be free.

George looks so small that night curled up in the undergrowth, surrounded by a jungle of sleeping flowers whose colours seem to glow in the moonlight.

He turns on his back and gazes upward.

The sky above looks richer than anything George has ever seen. But there is something more in that infinite world that holds him. It is the light of the stars, the heavens, the knowledge of which seems to bind him to the universe.

A single pick hits the hard earth twice.

They are spread out across the road, a chain gang rhythmically hitting the earth with their picks. Their bodies are linked by the clanking chains which deafen the air.

The road marked out ahead of them seems to go on forever.

The picks of the chain gang rise and fall, rise and fall, gradually losing their rhythm. We hear the voice of the guard McCallum:

MCCALLUM: Keep together!

The sounds are at odds with each other like the picks now slicing the sky.

But the guard is there with his:

> MCCALLUM: One, two. One, two. Keep together, you! One, two. One, two. One ... Come on, you lazy shower of shits. Put some muscle into that. D'you want the toe of my boot up your arsehole? One, two. One, two. One, two.

He pauses to see if his words have taken effect.

> MCCALLUM: If I catch any man shirking ...

He agitates the head of a whip protruding from his waist. The sounds are in unison. The guard wipes his brow with a rag, wipes the sweat from the back of his neck. He puts up his hand, winces at the sun dazzling blindingly down. He makes for the shade of his hut, a bit like a sentry-box on wheels.

> MCCALLUM: And don't look at me like that ... you'll be eating your own shit for breakfast or my name's not McCallum.

As he opens the door he is met by the guard dog. His face

beams with pleasure as the dog leaps up.

MCCALLUM: Stay in, Soldier, stay in boy. It's cooler.

McCallum has no compunction about closing the door to his hut, for although there are no windows, there is a peephole in the wood, an extracted hole. Inside McCallum holds out a fleshy chicken bone towards the dog. But first he wants the animal to perform a few tricks.

MCCALLUM: Take it nice.

Sure enough the dog gets up on its hind legs, then licks his face. But the giver wants more.

MCCALLUM: C'mon, take it nicely.

He lifts the bone higher to tantalize the creature. Suddenly the dog snaps at him.

MCCALLUM: Ah, you bastard! Bite me, would you? Bite me, you bastard!

In a flash the man goes for the dog, which sneaks out of sight in a corner.

McCallum moves lower so that he can take a peep through the hole.

As the picks hit the stony earth, a burly Convict is using the beat to verse his feelings:

CONVICT: If I ever meet up with him back home,
I'll show him where my foot will roam.
It won't be where it ought to be,
but up his arse and all for free.

He casts a concerned eye at the convict further along the line whom we recognize as Brine. But Brine looks the worse for wear, as if his body is moving in spite of him.

CONVICT: Keep with us, Brine. Don't let this bastard road be our memorial.

Poor Brine is beyond responding. He downs his foot on the shovel and sways in pain. His feet, swathed in blood-soaked rags, have a deformed look. We can hear a voice saying, 'Water, somebody.' Brine looks as if he is about to give in. The Convict shouts:

CONVICT: Water!

But Brine hits the ground.

The Guard throws open the door of his hut. He sizes up the atmosphere. He saunters across with a flask in his hand.

MCCALLUM: Who shouted?

The Convict wipes his dry mouth.

CONVICT: He needs his boots.

McCallum looks down, then up, sneering slightly.

MCCALLUM: He says somebody stole them . . .

McCallum comes to rest where Brine is lying at his feet. He considers the flask as if testing it for the measure of its contents. He takes a long slug and spews it.

MCCALLUM: Let him steal another pair.

The water trickles down Brine's forehead in small rivulets. It gathers in the crest of his eye before running down the side of his nose. He opens an eye

but all he can see is the rough earth with the ants gathering. They cluster in strength around a twig. They bear it up and take it away like a coffin.

That night, the chain gang are huddled up outside, totally exhausted, bundled together for warmth. In the encampment their shackles are removed. One of their number is playing softly on a mouth-organ.

Brine is there listening. The sentimental sound evokes a further sadness in him for it is the same tune that Elvi sang. The Convict leans across the prostrate Brine. He pulls back his hair to look into his face and whispers:

CONVICT: Are you all right Brine?

There is no answer. The Convict clasps Brine's shoulder tight.

A sound of raucous laughter. Behind the window of the drinking place we can see McCallum and his cronies. They are in the company of women. They are in high spirits. McCallum leads a Woman out of the door. He is somewhat tipsy and she has to put her hands on his hips to guide him towards a deep shadow. They seem to land themselves for we can hear them snuffling.

An immediate sound causes Brine to turn.

The Convict is covering his head with his shirt the way a woman might with a shawl. Brine looks curious. He whispers:

BRINE: You remind me of Ned Ludd.

CONVICT: Who was he?

BRINE: He became a she when he went machine-breaking.

We can hear the couple groaning. Deep in the shadows the Woman is heard saying:

WOMAN: You shouldn't drink so much.

Her answer is an incoherent grunt.

WOMAN: Can't you try a bit harder?

McCallum burps.

WOMAN: You can't do anything with that.

More grunts.

The Convict is watching and listening intently. He moves slightly but it is sufficient for Brine to be on the alert. Seeing him move again, he pulls him into the shadow next to him and whispers urgently:

BRINE: Whatever you do, don't do it alone. One man is nothing, I've learned that. We're here to help each other.

CONVICT: Go to sleep.

With that he goes. Brine watches him disappear.

Out of the silence the Woman complains:

WOMAN: Get down a bit. Have you never been with a woman before?

Sound of a body collapsing in a heap. The Woman emerges from the shadows, or rather stumbles for she is not too sober herself. She counts her money, clinking it. She continues across the shaft of light, going towards the gate. A voice asks her to declare herself.

WOMAN: Feel like a nice time, Bertie?

Screech of the gate opening.

WOMAN: No? There's not a man among you.

The gate closes behind her.

Elsewhere, a figure scampers across the shaft of light and into the long shadows.

Brine watches. Back inside the shadows there is no sound to be heard.

Finally the figure makes her appearance. As she approaches the lesser shadow of the gate, the Guard is heard calling:

GUARD: Wait!

Brine covers his eyes with his hands.

The Guard considers the figure, sizes her up and down. He seems to like what he sees.

GUARD: How much?

The figure shrugs, puts up four fingers. The guard thinks about that.

GUARD: Too much!

Brine lowers his hands.

The Convict, dressed as a whore, walks free.

The gate screeches shut behind him as he disappears along the road, his footsteps quickening the smaller he gets. With skirts held high he scampers across the wasteland like a figure in a pantomime.

In daylight, the Convict is dragged naked between two guards.

His hands are manacled to a stake.

The men are standing there as observers.

Brine has his head inside his chest, determined not to watch. He is confronted by McCallum, sensing his presence rather than being conscious of it. A flower touches his chest, slides up until the petals reach his nostrils.

MCCALLUM: Don't you like to be entertained?

Brine doesn't flinch. After an ominous pause

McCallum walks into the clearing. He flexes himself the way a weightlifter might. All around him seem to be holding their breath. He has his audience. He removes the whip from inside the top of his trousers. He takes up a ridiculous stance like a contorted circus performer. He swings himself round with a violent thrust. The lash cuts the light. His fist jolts. He relaxes. It was only a rehearsal.

94

One of his colleagues averts his eyes, while another manages to see the funny side.

This time McCallum adds sound to his ritual dance with a scream fit to burst his lungs. A sound that is only topped by the sound of the lash meeting its target.

Blood splatters across the sand.

The chain gang is back on the road, their picks swinging rhythmically against the sun as it rises low in the sky.

Once again McCallum has retired to his hut.

Inside, the dog is contentedly watching McCallum, who is sitting in the semi-darkness rubbing his crotch. He offers his free hand to the dog who licks it.

   MCCALLUM: Who's my pal? I could go for you. Come on, Soldier, come on.

The Convict glances over his shoulder at the hut. He catches Brine's attention and points upwards. He curves his finger indicating the way the sun is moving, then at

the shadow made by the hut, which is as it would be with the sun on a slant almost directly in front of it.

Brine shakes his head as if to say, 'Don't do anything.'

In the hut, McCallum is engrossed with his dog.

   MCCALLUM: That's my boy, that's it. Good dog, good boy, good Soldier, good Soldier!

The Convict whispers to his neighbour on the other side. He to the next and so on down the line.

A blazing sun.

The men at work, their picks slicing the earth. They are now very close to the hut.

As we see the hut now, the shadow is directly behind it and the sun is directly piercing the peephole.

Inside, lulled by the sound of the picks playing in unison, a shaft of sunlight throws a circle of light on McCallum's chest.

Suddenly the dog is watchful, agitated, whines.

McCallum starts, but the source of light is too much for his eye and he quickly withdraws from the peephole, dazzled by the sun.

There is no sound now. On the wall opposite, there is a split-second upside-down image of what is going on outside. We can see as in a camera obscura the figures of the men, quite still, poised.

Outside, the men have encircled the hut. Picks are raised.

Suddenly all hell is let loose as the picks descend and we hear the wood splitting.

The faces and arms of the men possess an energy perhaps they never knew existed within them.

The walls of the hut cave in.

The dog rushes out all yelping between their legs and

bolts for freedom across the landscape.

Silence.

The chain gang is nowhere to be seen. There is nothing in sight except the hacked-up road and what is left of the hut, a few stray pieces of wood and a couple of rusty hinges.

There is nothing to be heard except for the high-pitched whine of birds of prey in the distance.

We see the skeleton of the dead guard left by the vultures.

———————

It is the same location. Earth is being shovelled from a hole in the ground. A plain wooden coffin contains the skeleton's remains. Two convicts are digging the grave. The one at the top is resting, hearing the straining breathlessness from beneath.

DIGGER: If you dig any deeper, you'll reach England.

He laughs as the digging accelerates. The shovel is flung free. A hand appears in a gesture for help. The digger pulls out his companion.

Old Stanfield looks a pale reflection of his former self.

A pair of officials stand waiting near a carriage, where a Union Jack has been unravelled. The two are in whispered consultation, before one of them turns.

OFFICIAL: You!

No reaction.

OFFICIAL: You there!

Old Stanfield and his companion digger are waiting by the side of the grave. They look up.

OFFICIAL: Yes, you.

Old Stanfield's companion digger moves forward.

OFFICIAL: Not you, you imbecile.

They stand there looking momentarily ridiculous.

The Official makes an aside to his neighbour:

OFFICIAL: Don't they understand plain English?

The other smothers a smile. The Official smacks his leg.

The face of Old Stanfield. We see that his hair has turned white as he lowers his head, clasps his hands together.

OLD STANFIELD: Our Father which art in heaven, hallowed

97

be thy name. Thy kingdom come, thy will be done as it is in heaven...

He is presiding over the coffin draped with the flag, made to resume his role as minister over the proceedings. He is saying the Lord's Prayer with his own simplicity and feeling:

OLD STANFIELD: Give us this day our daily bread, and forgive us our debts as we forgive our debtors. Lead us not into temptation but deliver us from evil. For thine is the kingdom, the power and the glory, for ever and ever. Amen.

On their way back, the two convicts sit on top of the carriage with the driver. They are back to back, Old Stanfield lulled by the shaking of the vehicle. His companion digger is sitting there lost in his own thoughts, but he turns to look at the Union Jack protruding from a rucksack. Beside it their shovels are lying where an old newspaper has been laid out. He inclines his head at an awkward angle to read

a news item. We catch the words LONDON–DORCHESTER COMMITTEE. It seems that in England there is some agitation for the release of the Union men.

The carriage is jogging too much to go on reading. The digger is not interested anyway and Old Stanfield is oblivious.

The carriage enters an estate. From the door of the gate house, a gentleman sentry watches them go through.

The landscape drifting by at the side of the driveway is formal but free. Turning a corner we catch a glimpse of an aboriginal reservation. The people are standing outside their huts content to watch the carriage passing. Surrounding them as if to mark their location is a circle of trees. As free as they appear, there is something sad about their faces.

Finally we settle on the residence, of the grand colonial type and symmetrical like the formal gardens before it.

Inside the drawing room we find a figure cutting something out of black paper. He has his back to us. He glances up at

Mr Norfolk, posed by the window, giving of his best profile.

The Silhouettist speaks with a French accent:

SILHOUETTIST: Tell me something more about yourself, for identification, monsieur.

Mr Norfolk nods.

NORFOLK: I was born William Moncrieff Norfolk on New Year's Day, 1790, educated at Harrow and Oxford, commanded a regiment at Waterloo, great times! I came to New South Wales as Governor of this province...

The Silhouettist is still recovering from the tactless reference to Waterloo, but continues with the task in hand. While Mr Norfolk grows more and more confiding:

NORFOLK: My wife finds the climate here oppressive, suffers from the vapours. Longs to return to Grantham, pines pathetically for the values of the mother country. Women are happier at home, of course. They shouldn't meddle in the outside world.

He glances towards the window.

NORFOLK: Our daughter Flower's adapted rather better. She's taken to horses. She'll make an excellent marriage one day.

The Silhouettist blinks at this piece of English logic, but it is as nothing compared to Mr Norfolk's next confidence.

NORFOLK: I sometimes feel the urge to have more children, a son, but my wife and I ... it's like a square peg in a round hole.

The Silhouettist's eye widens in disbelief.

NORFOLK: Now I regard the subjects of this province as my family. I'm a martyr to duty, public service, diplomacy. I think it's generally acknowledged that I have promoted a measure of stability where before there was none.

The Silhouettist flicks the scissors away from himself in a theatrical gesture, indicating that he has almost finished the cutting.

SILHOUETTIST: Merci, monsieur. It is obvious you possess a very liberal turn of mind, a quality that is greatly appreciated in my country.

He is becoming more loquacious:

SILHOUETTIST: You will of course be familiar with *les raisons d'être* of the French Revolution?

Snip-snip go the scissors as he cuts off the head at the collar.

SILHOUETTIST: *Liberté, égalité, fraternité.*

Snip-snip. With some professionalism he flutters about laying the silhouette on white paper. A sound of the door opening.

Charlie, George Loveless's small companion, is standing at the door, tray in hand, dressed like an old-fashioned blackamoor.

CHARLIE: Your apertive, sir.

He moves forward.

SILHOUETTIST: *Apéritif*!

The Silhouettist waves his hand in exasperation as Charlie almost lands his glass on the newly finished silhouette.

SILHOUETTIST: *Sacré bleu*!

He signals Charlie away and snatches up his work.

The silhouette in relief on its background of white paper is a distinctly flattering portrait of Mr Norfolk.

A relaxed Norfolk nods approval, perhaps with a touch of vanity for his reputation. From outside there comes the distant sound of a young girl giggling. Norfolk turns the same profile to the window.

Outside, Flower, the Governor's daughter, is sitting astride a tiny Shetland pony. Old Stanfield, leading the pony by the reins, is taking the child on her outing. She strokes the animal affectionately, offering it endearing words, then:

FLOWER: Why don't you tell me another of your wonderful stories, Stanfield?

Old Stanfield looks at her doubtfully.

OLD STANFIELD: I don't think I know any more.

FLOWER: But you must. You promised me.

She laughs high-spiritedly.

FLOWER: I know you are pretending.

They have continued their walkabout and come to stop at a place where Flower observes

The Aborigine reservation. The people there are as distant from her as she is from them.

On their way back through the formal gardens, Flower complains:

FLOWER: I don't always understand what Jesus says, do you? If Pappa said such things, he would become a laughing stock, wouldn't he?

She looks like an old woman with her head leaning on her chest. She sighs the deepest of sighs.

Old Stanfield considers her for a moment, no doubt wondering how on earth he can get through to her. He turns his eyes away and says out of the blue:

OLD STANFIELD: I have a daughter just about your age.

The child looks at him as much as to say, 'How could such a thing be possible?' She obviously resents his familiarity.

Flower places her foot in the cleft of Old Stanfield's worn hand and steps down on to gravel.

She proceeds towards the house, but retraces her steps back to a puddle. She splashes in it, then continues on her way calling out her reminder:

FLOWER: You won't forget to clean my shoes.

That evening, Old Stanfield's face looks angry, glowers, grows dark with fury. He is sitting at a table in his quarters.

On closer inspection we can see he is perusing well-thumbed books of a religious nature. At least one of them has a crucifix embedded in the leather. He is going from book to book as if he is searching for something appropriate. He fumbles with the books in front of him but chucks them aside as useless.

The Aborigines are gathered together rather like a missionary class. They either stand or crouch. Several of them, probably the leaders, are denoted by painted markings like a skeleton. The place is silent. Old Stanfield is crouched before them.

OLD STANFIELD: We have only ourselves.

Out of the crowd the solitary face of a lone Aborigine.

OLD STANFIELD: We must help one another. One man is strong. United among other men, he is stronger.

All of them enclosed by the circle of trees.

OLD STANFIELD: You must learn to read and write and think for yourselves.

There is no indication whether his audience understands or not.

OLD STANFIELD: You must use this...

He points to his head.

OLD STANFIELD: Not this...

He clenches his fist, then encloses the fist with his other hand.

OLD STANFIELD: If we fight among ourselves, we please our masters . . .

He glances at

The Governor's residence.

OLD STANFIELD: We perpetuate our serfdom. Because they know we will never stand together against them. They like us to be stupid. That is why they don't educate us.

He falls silent.

The black faces look quite blank.

Mr Norfolk taps the newspaper, sitting behind his desk in his study next day.

NORFOLK: You have become quite famous, Mr Stanfield, quite the celebrity. People in high places are championing your cause. I envy you. You should read about yourself.

He hands over the paper, gets up and moves away.

We find him standing by the window in a pose similar to that of the Silhouettist.

NORFOLK: Tell me. What is this . . . this Society of Friends, the wisdom of which you are so eager to bestow upon others . . .

He glances out of the window.

NORFOLK: . . . to whom, I may say, I have already extended the hand of friendship. Perhaps you would wish to share it with me.

He turns and casts a teasing eye in the direction of Old Stanfield.

NORFOLK: I am, as you know, as indeed all must know, a fair man. Why, I will talk to anyone who will listen to me.

His gesture is as large as the room.

Old Stanfield continues to stand in silence. Suddenly Norfolk grabs the paper out of his hands.

NORFOLK: You won't read about yourself?

He offers him a quick impatient face, and resumes his seat behind his desk.

NORFOLK: You should.

He relegates the newspaper to one side. He moves the one untidy object on his desk to restore the symmetry. Then he sits back, his hands clasped together, to consider Old Stanfield. His voice changes its tone.

NORFOLK: Mr Stanfield. We are not uneducated men, are we?

OLD STANFIELD: The field was my university.

The old man looks as plain as the field he is describing.

Norfolk is disconcerted for a moment, but draws breath and decides to start again:

NORFOLK: Stanfield. I respect your homespun philosophy but I cannot have you preaching insurrection.

Norfolk pauses to let that take effect.

This is the world into which our young blackamoor emerges. He looks around as if he senses all is not well. The two men are static. Charlie goes nervously towards the desk with his tray to remove a sherry glass and decanter. Norfolk looks put out but carries on.

NORFOLK: The native population are little more than savages ... in spite of my efforts to rescue them from extinction. Surely you must recognize the impropriety of . . .

He waves his hand about searching for the right word:

NORFOLK: . . . arousing them.

Old Stanfield, lost in deep thought, is oblivious to Charlie's ministrations. When he speaks it comes from honest conviction:

OLD STANFIELD: I know that we are all God's children.

There is a beseeching look in his eyes. He lowers his head in a modest way. But instead of looking pious it has the opposite effect. One of victory.

Charlie knocks over the glass. There is no sound save for a gentle clink. Its contents spoil the newspaper. Charlie tries using his sleeve to clean up the mess which only makes matters worse.

Norfolk looks as stunned as if he suddenly had egg on his face. Instantly all hell is let loose, with a loud crash and a shout from Norfolk.

NORFOLK: You imbecile!

He looks beside himself with rage, with temper so vivid it scorches his face.

NORFOLK: You snivelling workhouse guttersnipe! How dare you . . .

Old Stanfield looks alarmed

for Charlie, who is at the mercy of Norfolk's wrath.

NORFOLK: How dare you fetch your filthy stench to foul the air, you contaminating labouring scab! Get out . . .

But Charlie can't because Norfolk has him by the ear.

NORFOLK: Get out before I send you back where you belong, inside your whore's belly.

Norfolk's voice rampages down the empty hallway as Flower makes her entrance. Knowing better than to proceed further she comes to a halt, about turns and tiptoes back the way she came. She has no sooner gone out the door than

Charlie charges out and across the hall as if death was imminent, his body motivated by Norfolk's continued castigations.

Outside, as the door crashes behind him, Charlie collides with the unsuspecting Flower

sending her into a puddle.

Flower's pony turns to consider her. But her yells of protestation don't disturb him too much as he goes straight back to munching his hay.

A kangaroo lifts its docile head.

Charlie scampers across the wilderness.

The kangaroo leaps across a clearing.

Charlie has come to a forest. He looks dirty and footsore. He turns his blackamoor's uniform inside out but the thorns have seared right through giving him a ragged look not unlike a clown. He rubs the blacking from his face. He stops to consider the road ahead. A difficult decision for this is where three paths meet. A figure emerges from the distance, striding along, coming towards Charlie. Catching sight of the boy he waves. He looks like a total stranger.

At closer range we see his hair has been cut and his eyes, though friendly, have a haunted look about them. To outward appearances he looks like another convict. It is in fact Young Stanfield. He slows down. Being the country bumpkin at heart he nods a:

YOUNG STANFIELD: How-dy.

and comes to a stop.

Poor Charlie looks rooted to the spot, with one leg poised awkwardly behind him as if to give himself a start.

Young Stanfield looks away and nods indicating the world he has emerged from. It stretches to the horizon without any visible sign of human life. It looks more like another planet.

YOUNG STANFIELD: I was beginning to think there were no more people living in the world.

He looks a lonely individual standing there.

YOUNG STANFIELD: You're the first person I've seen in a week.

He appears to be talking to himself. When a squawk of birds interrupts the silence he glances up as if grateful for the sound of something alive.

YOUNG STANFIELD: I'm making for the Governor's country residence.

Charlie's face looks wild and somewhat wary, with his hair practically standing on end. He moves his head, moves his body forward on a curve as if frightened of passing too close. Young Stanfield is aware of his movement without turning.

CHARLIE: Have you got anything to eat?

Young Stanfield shakes his head sympathetically.

Charlie, who but for a few steps would be on a line with the stranger, doesn't look too convinced. He clutches on to his stomach as if letting go would make it worse.

Young Stanfield's rucksack hits the dust.

YOUNG STANFIELD: Here, see for yourself.

The pack remains.

Young Stanfield glances towards the forest, the direction from which Charlie has come. Charlie points to the third path ahead of him.

CHARLIE: You want to go that way.

Young Stanfield glances in that direction uncertainly.

YOUNG STANFIELD: Which way are you going?

Charlie repeats the gesture.

CHARLIE: That way.

The boy lowers his head. When he finally hears Young Stanfield ask:

YOUNG STANFIELD: Where have you come from?

Charlie boringly points in the direction of the forest without giving it the benefit of his eyes.

CHARLIE: That way.

Young Stanfield smothers a smile.

A satisfied Charlie lumbers himself with the rucksack and away the two of them go, taking the third path to who knows where. However, on the way Young Stanfield can't resist a look back and by the way he hesitates he doesn't look entirely convinced.

YOUNG STANFIELD: Why are you going so fast?

Charlie turns impatiently.

CHARLIE: Want to get there, don't you?

Charlie is beckoning him on with perhaps a fraction more than total confidence. As they fall into line Charlie rests his hand on the other's shoulder, and there they go looking for all the world like two old friends, Charlie even managing to whistle a hint of a merry tune.

But that night they have arrived nowhere. Young Stanfield sits cross-legged by a makeshift fire while Charlie huddles almost hidden neath his companion's blanket.

YOUNG STANFIELD: I'm going to see my father. I haven't seen him in three years.

Silence.

YOUNG STANFIELD: Don't fret now, we'll find something to eat tomorrow. When I get home I'll not go hungry again, that's for sure. I'll forget about this place. No child of mine shall ever know what I've been through.

Transfixed by the flames, Young Stanfield starts to fantasize.

YOUNG STANFIELD: Now if I was Lord Mayor, I'd get rid of the old way of life. There'd be no more bowing and scraping.

We'd build a new world. D'you hear me, Charlie?

But Charlie has gone to sleep.

YOUNG STANFIELD: Oh well . . .

He uses his stick to scatter the embers.

CHARLIE: Look!

Next day, Charlie is astride Young Stanfield's shoulders, pointing excitedly at –

a profusion of orange trees.

Young Stanfield's ravenous hand plucks an orange –

and passes it to Charlie. He takes another for himself and digs his jowls into its juicy flesh.

YOUNG STANFIELD: That's beautiful. Good, eh?

CHARLIE: Mmm.

They are luxuriating in their world of plenty. If only it could always be like this.

To sounds of merriment, Charlie's upstretched hand relieves the branches of their fruit.

YOUNG STANFIELD: See them up there? They're the biggest.

One by one they tumble as if it were harvest time. Charlie yells with delight, perched high on his companion's shoulders.

YOUNG STANFIELD: That's a boy. A few more . . .

The earth is covered with more oranges than they could possibly consume.

Judging by the amount of peel surrounding them, they have eaten more than their fill. It has certainly taken its toll on Young Stanfield who, protective hand to his stomach, eyes closed, head lolling almost drunkenly back against the ground, looks pleasantly bloated. He dozes off.

Charlie's hands move stealthily towards Young Stanfield's rucksack.

The silence is ominous. Some sixth sense has Young Stanfield looking about himself. He could be a character out of a fairy tale wondering if he has been dreaming all this. He closes his eyes and opens them. No, he isn't dreaming. There's no Charlie and no bag. He gets to his feet and glances round apprehensively. He calls out sharply:

YOUNG STANFIELD: Charlie?

And yet again, wandering up and down the rows of bushes:

YOUNG STANFIELD: Charlie?

Silence.

A hand, a strange hand, reaches to pluck an orange. There is something uncanny in its way of taking. It has a savouring quality of possession about it. As the hand twists and turns a bejewelled finger catches the sunlight and glints.

An innocent Young Stanfield calls out again:

YOUNG STANFIELD: Charlie?

The orange rolls into his path.

Young Stanfield sees the joke and smiles. With a playful shout he goes in search of the invisible Charlie.

On turning the corner his face falls.

Before him on the ground lie the scattered contents of his rucksack.

Suddenly, looming towards him, like something out of a nightmare, comes a rider on horseback.

Then another.

And yet another, the earth pounding with hoofs of war.

In a flash Young Stanfield finds himself roped and dragged into a clearing. He is being manhandled by three horsemen, two of whom dismount and set about him.

From horseback, the Fop looks down disdainfully. Unable to bear the screams, Charlie lowers his head in shame. He can do nothing. He is saddled neatly in the Fop's crotch. An object of possession.

The riders veer off through the trees.

Young Stanfield has been abandoned. He has been staked to the ground, rendering him immovable.

He can utter nothing for an orange has been rammed in his gaping mouth.

There is just the sight of the trees as the sound of the invaders dwindles to nothing.

But it has all been observed by the lone Aborigine crouching in a tree.

His feet drop down to the dusty ground and he pads across to stop

above the prostrate and terrified figure of Young Stanfield.

Tears course down the lone Aborigine's cheeks.

———————————————

An ear-piercing whistle. It is a bit like the moment before the beginning of the world. We see a vast landscape, stretching out as rich as a peacock's fan. There are hundreds of sheep, their constant mewing filling the air to near exclusion of all else.

Several riders and dogs are rounding them up, circling the perimeter. We can hear the hoofs and the riders' shrill whistles.

We see the animals in a stranglehold as they press forward or try to, for they are locked against each other in a way that appears static to the eye, almost as if they don't know which way to turn, some of them facing in the wrong direction.

One of the riders makes a swift turn. It is Mrs Carlyle, her golden hair flying carelessly free, her sheer physicality born of the earth, her face – held now – exhilarated.

Then the sheep surge forward as a breed with a tremendous release of energy. We watch them career across the landscape, and marvel at the skill of the herdsmen.

That evening, outside the stables at Mrs Carlyle's homestead, we hear a cheerful tune played on a Jew's harp. The player says, 'Night, mam' as he goes and Mrs Carlyle thanks him for a good day's work. She is clearly on friendly terms with her employees, referring to him as 'Samuel'. Samuel leaves with one or two others, losing himself and his tune in the shadows.

Clutching a hank of straw firmly in her fist, Mrs Carlyle busies herself grooming her horse.

Inside the stable the last of the herdsmen is washing himself down. He is stripped to the waist, washing his torso. Small rivulets of water course silently down his skin. There is something attractive about his lean muscularity or so it seems for

Mrs Carlyle is there, watching him intently. The place is silent

but for the sound of water trickling down. Save for her constant gaze, there is a remoteness about Mrs Carlyle, a void.

Lost in himself till now, the herdsman glances round, the way one does feeling watched. It is here we recognize James Loveless, looking grizzled and worn, but ruddy from the outdoor life. He turns away, offers a sideways look, if anything more a feeling of awareness than a look.

JAMES: I'll say goodnight then, mam.

Inside the living room, Mrs Carlyle is greeted by her dog. She runs her hand smoothly over the animal in a caressing way. The creature licks her hand and, satisfied, settles down.

MRS CARLYLE: Tell me, James, have you been happy here? Working for me?

James is standing by the door, feeling somewhat self-conscious.

JAMES: Yes, I've been happy enough, Mrs Carlyle.

She cuts in:

MRS CARLYLE: 'Mrs Carlyle', 'Mrs Carlyle'. My name is Violet.

JAMES: Yes, mam.

Mrs Carlyle tries to appear bright but it is a brightness born out of anxiety. She makes a show of relaxing, we feel in order to alleviate her own situation as much as to impress James. Removing her jacket she reveals her woman's clothing.

MRS CARLYLE: Do you know, ever since my husband ... Do you know, I never heard my name in three whole years. I was prepared to think I never had one.

She lets out a throaty laugh. She swings back her head so that her hair cascades. What was at first an almost masculine look of authority is now a face of sultry beauty. She runs her fingers round the neckline of her blouse, as if by accident laying her shoulder bare.

MRS CARLYLE: Have you ever thought, James, to make yourself a life out here? This country has a lot to offer for a man like you.

She substantiates her remark with an incredulous sweeping gesture of the hand.

MRS CARLYLE: How should I have managed without you?

James is quite still. Somewhere on the wall behind him we can see a portrait of Mrs Carlyle's husband in a mourning frame.

MRS CARLYLE: I could see to it that you had every opportunity. I could arrange for your wife and children to join you.

She tilts her head hopefully.

JAMES: I am childless.

Mrs Carlyle looks like the saddest person in the world.

MRS CARLYLE: It's a terrible thing to be alone with oneself.

We have the feeling that any moment she will burst into tears. She stares at her open palm.

MRS CARLYLE: I do wish you'd consider it.

Then, with resignation:

MRS CARLYLE: I'm not getting any younger.

The words seem to have struck a chord in James.

JAMES: I love my wife.

James quietly puts on his shirt. He turns his back on her.

Mrs Carlyle turns to look at her dog. She taps her lap invitingly.

But the animal remains.

When she taps her lap again it is in a sort of self-comforting way. She takes out a letter, an open one, its seal undone, from a drawer in her desk and fingers it almost playfully.

MRS CARLYLE: I shall be sorry to lose you.

She lifts up the letter and holds it forth. She moves her hand forward for the thing to be taken but it remains in her grasp.

MRS CARLYLE: This is from your brother.

JAMES: George?

Overcome, he covers his mouth with his hand and flops down on to a chair. It is as if having waited until now he suddenly has all the time in the world. The letter is probably the most tantalizing thing he has ever seen, but the suspense he has created for himself proves too much and he remains there, a figure of abject sadness.

The silence unsettles Mrs Carlyle, and she clears her throat. She peruses the letter for a moment then, half turned away, she reads its contents by the beam of a lamp.

MRS CARLYLE: 'My dearest brother, I pray to God my

message reaches you at last. I have tried all manner of means, but hearing nothing from you I feared the worst.'

She looks momentarily uncomfortable knowing perhaps she should have revealed the letter before.

MRS CARLYLE: 'It gladdens my heart to alert you to news of our freedom. The good Lord has looked into the hearts of men and shown them that, imperfect as we are, we did never countenance violence nor any violation of the law. Good friends at home have rallied to our cause and argued long and hard on our behalf. Rejoice, my long lost brother, in the free pardon granted to us. See to it that you complete your work to the best of your ability, that our time here may be said to be honestly done.'

She turns briefly, the way one might feeling alone.

An open mountainous landscape by day. James has set off on his trek and can be seen taking the long high road. We hear the voice of Mrs Carlyle read out the rest of the letter:

MRS CARLYLE: 'We shall all be waiting to welcome you, all save Hammett of whom there is no trace. Fear not, brother, He that is for us is more than all that is against us. We will, we will, we will be free. Your ever loving brother, George Loveless.'

He becomes a speck on the horizon and in a moment disappears from view.

The sweep of the earth looks barren and lifeless until we come to a solitary shack. On closer inspection, the place looks derelict. Still, it is not without a semblance of something for its gaping holes have been filled, if somewhat makeshift, against the elements. A sound of braying leads us further, to a donkey attached to a small box-like wagon. Finally there are sounds of splashing water and an Italian aria.

We see a grizzled old man beside a lake. He is busily washing a plate of glass. He keeps looking at it expectantly and muttering to himself incessantly.

MAD PHOTOGRAPHER: Come on, come clean for me.

He squints up at a dazzling sun on its way to a cloud.

MAD PHOTOGRAPHER: *Si, si, bella bella bellisima.*

He hurries away.

When we next encounter him, he is manoeuvering the lone Aborigine across an open patch of ground.

MAD PHOTOGRAPHER: You come with me. I take your image. I take image of you, you understand? Come, come, I show you.

The bewildered Aborigine, reluctant at first, finally lets him take him. But this may be because his assailant is muttering endless gibberish, besides his appearance, which is dauntingly eccentric. He is operatic in the full sense of the word.

MAD PHOTOGRAPHER: You stand here, very still, understand, like so . . .

He fixes the Aborigine up against a tree with a twig as clamp, and satisfied that his captive is where he wants him, he backtracks in order to survey him.

MAD PHOTOGRAPHER: Good, good, good.

Returning once more he moves the man's head slightly. The poor Aborigine looks as if he is about to be executed.

MAD PHOTOGRAPHER: *Molto belli.* This is so good. Don't move.

In his excitement the old man kisses his subject on both cheeks.

The camera, when we discover it, is like no camera we have ever seen before. The Mad Photographer puts his head beneath a dark cover to focus on

the Aborigine, but into his upside-down view inadvertently strays James Loveless.

MAD PHOTOGRAPHER: *Jesu bambino*! Get away. You, go away. Move, move.

A stunned James proceeds to move back and forth like an idiot. Unfortunately the Aborigine thinks the order is meant for him.

MAD PHOTOGRAPHER: No, no, no, no. Stay still. No, you get away.

The Mad Photographer's hands, but not his head, emerge wildly flailing. Quite clearly the world is made up of fools.

MAD PHOTOGRAPHER: You stay but you move.

Finally James retreats and all is set to right. The old man surfaces and dabs the sweat from his brow.

MAD PHOTOGRAPHER: Stay very still.

He takes out his fob watch. He glances upward. He moves his free hand above the brass plunger.

MAD PHOTOGRAPHER: *Dieci, nove, otto, sette, sei, cinque, quattro, tre, due, UNO!*

He pushes the silent plunger.

He waits there for a second like a face that has seen the muse. When the bang comes it is no more than a pip and a squeak.

While out of the machine in all directions issues steam. In next to no time his world is rendered invisible.

Meanwhile James forces open the door to the shack. It opens just enough to let him squeeze through.

The room is dark inside. He gropes around. At first there is just the tinkle of glass then the crash of it as it falls. He grapples with a curtain to let the sun come streaming in. The place is filled with dozens of glass plates hanging on lines, crazy optical apparatus and bottles of chemicals.

An image of the photographer on one of the plates dissolves silently to nothing.

The light penetrates another image of the photographer's donkey and it too disappears.

James is mesmerized. He turns with all the innocence of a child and there before him, wonder of wonders, is Hammett, caught for a magical instant in time.

JAMES: Hammett!

James speaks in a whisper. If only he could reach him, if only the image could become substance. But Hammett fades away like a lamented goodbye.

The Mad Photographer wrenches open the door.

MAD PHOTOGRAPHER: *Jesu! Jesu!*

He is frothing at the mouth. He raises his hand in horror.

The suddenness so alarms James, he topples shelving to the floor with a great shattering of glass.

The would-be inventor goes berserk.

MAD PHOTOGRAPHER: Idiot, idiot. My invention, what do you do? You destroy my work. *Assassino!*

Pushing James out of the way, he grovels among the splinters to rescue vital parts. He mutters insanities. In due course he looks up hopelessly. The tragedy has rendered him mute. All is lost.

James scrambles out of the shack. He has wrecked the premature invention of photography and expediency being the better part of ignorance, he takes to the road in a hurry. Somewhere along the way he glances back.

The Aborigine is still there beneath the tree, transfixed, waiting.

––––––––––––––––

Beneath the branches of another tree wait four men, in silhouette. James approaches on a line with them. He moves quietly forward. We can feel the years stripping away as he progresses to meet them. He comes to a stop at the edge of the sheltering branches, is some time regarding his comrades, like one considering a mirage. He stretches out his hands. He smothers Brine in an embrace. His hands now go in a chain from one to the other, to Old Stanfield and his son. He folds them tightly in his arms. Finally there is George. They are like two awkward strangers standing there. Then they are content to hold on to one another. We wonder if they will ever let go.

––––––––––––––––

Weird demonic laughter, like the sound of a thousand bats descending, is coming from a witch-like creature, made more sinister by the beam of lantern light emitting from her crouching figure.

Turbulent white smoke against a dark sky. Gradually out of the smoke, a phantasmagoria, growing in proportion.

It seems to have mortified the audience, who in spite of their apparent elegance are shrinking back in terror.

The image being projected on to the smoke takes on mammoth proportions, amid the oohs and aahs of the audience. It is a skeleton.

Then suddenly it is gone. Darkness.

A light plays instead on the faces of the gratified crowd, who giggle and applaud, and toss their clinking coins

for the benefit of the old woman. Her spindly fingers reach out for the smattering of silver coins. The dainty feet of a woman in white pass and step over a prostrate body. Where she walks, the place seems to be littered with bodies, either lying immobile or drifting by like shadows in the flickering light. It could pass for a vision of hell. This is the dockside area where the wealthy come to slum.

Dim lights give promise of other dubious entertainments suggestive of the seamy underworld of the waterfront. There is a fairground atmosphere. We hear the sounds of attractions of one kind or another, of music and dance. An auctioneer is plying his trade.

>AUCTIONEER: Ladies and gentlemen, feast your eyes on that naked gleaming flesh. The arms, ladies and gentlemen, made for lifting heavy loads. The back, like a mule!

On a tumbril are a small group of anonymous convicts huddled together as if awaiting inspection. It is clear they have not just arrived for they have the gnarled and swarthy appearance of rejects or troublemakers, cast off by their previous owners.

>AUCTIONEER: Come now, ladies and gentlemen, you all look as if you could do with a little domestic assistance.

A group of ladies who seem to be on a sight-seeing tour. The woman in white opens her parasol and joins them, seeming to ingratiate herself with them.

>AUCTIONEER: Look at the torso, ladies and gentlemen, the biceps . . .

Hammett is standing there at the front of the platform. He doesn't look as if he is going anywhere. But then his wrists are tied together.

>AUCTIONEER: Ladies and gentlemen, what am I bid for this fine human specimen. What am I bid? He may be a bit rough and ready but treat him right I say and there's a hard day's work in him yet.

Hammett certainly looks as though he's been through a number of brawls, but his spirit is apparently unimpaired. He holds up his head and wears the very slightest of smirks on his face. He parades up and down a sort of catwalk, half brazen, half contemptuous.

>AUCTIONEER: Now come on, I want to hear the sound of

money, ladies and gentlemen.

The woman in white, perhaps led on by the ladies around her, bids:

WOMAN: Four shillings.

AUCTIONEER: Now there's a lady of measure.

A male voice from the crowd counterbids:

VOICE: Five shillings.

WOMAN: Six shillings.

VOICE: Seven shillings.

Hammett's eyes glance from side to side as the bidding goes on.

WOMAN: Eight shillings.

VOICE: Nine shillings.

Excitement rises.

The crowd has doubled in size.

AUCTIONEER: Dig deep into your pockets. I want to hear the jingle of coin. Is there any advance on seventeen shillings?

The woman in white waits like a born gambler.

VOICE: Eighteen.

A note of consternation from the crowd. The tension is at its height.

WOMAN: Nineteen.

She casts an eye in the direction of her opponent, apparently relishing the kind of pleasure that comes from competition. Her companions twitter with excitement.

AUCTIONEER: Do I hear a pound? Will anyone give me a round pound? Look at the muscles, ladies and gentlemen.

Finally the voice comes, firm but subdued with suppressed anger.

VOICE: One pound.

AUCTIONEER: Going for a pound. Going, going, gone for a pound. Thank you, sir.

The woman in white smothers a smile. She glances up from behind her parasol and offers a surreptitious wink to

The Auctioneer who rubs his nose in a business gesture.

The Fop pushes his way through the crowd, smirks with innocent satisfaction, and slaps his money down in the

Auctioneer's outstretched palm.

The tracks of a railway line by day seeming like something out
of a fairground.

We can hear the rumbling carriage as we ride through the trees.

In a single open-top wagon sit the Fop and Charlie, like his
catamite.

The railway is manpowered. Hammett is one of the four runners
manning the crossbars of the vehicle.

As they near the end of the flat run, they leap up on to the
pushbars and down the slope they go, for all the world like
pleasure-seekers at the funfair. The vehicle, carried by its own
velocity, sweeps the corner and disappears, its trundling sound
diminishing as it goes.

The wagon is now static where the railway line ends near a
police station. There are several armed guards in the vicinity.

Hammett is panting for breath but upright for all that. There is
a sort of defiance in him that won't let go.

HAMMETT: The bastard. He won't lick me. I'll see him in
hell first.

He glances at

Charlie who has been left sitting alone in the wagon.

HAMMETT: So how does it feel to join the nobility?

Charlie lowers his head as if in shame. He hears Hammett add:

HAMMETT: If you were old enough to know better, I'd chop
your balls off. There's one thing you don't do, son, and that's
turn against your own kind.

Hammett glances at the station house. One or two law enforcers
are mingling there in polite conversation with a lady of means.
They have a studied look about them, a posturing that is clearly
anathema to Hammett.

HAMMETT: There's some folks that think they're better than
others. They're not. Just more selfish, that's all.

He stares into space, deep in his own thoughts.

CHARLIE: What's your name?

HAMMETT: Out here I have no name.

Charlie tries again.

123

CHARLIE: Why are you here?

HAMMETT: I'm here instead of my brother.

He laughs, relaxes.

HAMMETT: What's the difference, we're all brothers.

He looks at his fellow runners, who are totally exhausted, either leaning on their bars or hanging over them. One is flat out on the ground.

CHARLIE: What did your brother do?

HAMMETT: He's a carpenter. A craftsman. If it wasn't for him and others like him, then everything would just fall apart.

He shakes his bar as if to prove his point and sure enough it drops slightly under his weight. He glances at the join to find a wedge has loosened itself.

CHARLIE: I mean what crime did he commit?

Hammett quietly manoeuvres the bar to see the wedge gradually slipping out.

HAMMETT: Him? Oh, he didn't do anything wrong. Just wanted folks to be treated right.

He ekes out the wedge and throws it down out of sight.

HAMMETT: He believed in what he was doing.

He looks out across the landscape.

HAMMETT: And out there, there's five others just like him. Now that I know what they've been through, I admire them. I count myself one of them.

The Fop emerges from the police station with an officer, toying with his pistol. Whatever they are talking about we can't tell but it looks like idle chatter.

Hammett watches with a look of vengeance.

HAMMETT: All my life people thought they owned me. But I'm free.

He presses his fist to his chest.

HAMMETT: In here, where it counts. I'm a free man.

Charlie is impressed by his sincerity.

HAMMETT: No matter how other men may treat you, they can never own your soul. Remember that.

The men re-assemble as the Fop steps up into the carriage, changing his position to face Charlie for the return journey.

Hands clench the bars and take the strain. They are on the move.

The figure of the officer becomes small.

The feet of the runners gather speed.

The wagon takes a curve and starts up the slope through an expanse of picturesque woodland.

The Fop smiles at Charlie. We hear the runners panting.

Hammett is putting every ounce of strength into it. The bar creaks as they strive to make the climb, inching forward. He eyes the top of the slope barely a few yards away. Almost instantly there is a sound of breaking

as the wood snaps.

The wagon holds for a moment, but only for a moment, then in one violent surge gravity takes the upper hand

and it falls away back down the slope at an accelerating speed.

The four runners scarper in all directions.

The Fop looks stultified with terror. He pulls out his pistol and tries to fire it, but it jumps out of his hand.

As they swerve beneath trees, Charlie sees his chance and grabs at an overhanging branch.

The wagon circles the trees and disappears from view. With a noisy screech it leaves the rails and capsizes somewhere out of sight.

A yell from Charlie causes Hammett to turn round and stop in mid-flight. He looks as if he is totally torn between making sure of his escape or risking his chance to rescue the boy.

Charlie is hanging perilously on a branch until Hammett comes to lift him down.

Charlie struggles out of his grasp and runs for his life, to the accompaniment of Hammett's ironic laughter.

He laughs as though he had never laughed before.

The twin doors of the police station burst open to reveal the incoming Fop. He comes trussed up like some mutilated scarecrow on crutches. The officer comes to his aid, but he fobs him off with a perpendicular wave of one of his crutches. He crashes the wooden supports on top of the officer's desk and seats himself. Behind his bandages, he looks like a tiger out for the kill.

In another part of the room, the officer considers the prisoner, lying flat on his back with his head pushed down between banisters. He looks like one at the end of his tether.

OFFICER: So, comrade. Are you going to tell us your name or aren't you?

Hammett, a truculent face.

HAMMETT: Free man.

He pauses. He has been badly beaten up.

HAMMETT: My name is Adam Freeman.

The officer puts in the boot.

He crosses to his desk, once more the efficient bureaucrat.

OFFICER: Now, you just sign this transportation order and I'll give you a receipt.

A paper is furnished before the Fop. He glowers over it, takes off his glove and signs it with relish.

OFFICER: He'll be sent to the penal settlement on Norfolk Island.

He savours his words.

OFFICER: The dwelling of devils in human form. The refuse of Botany Bay. The doubly damned.

He adds for good measure:

OFFICER: He'd be better off dead.

The Fop's eyes gleam with gratitude. He seals the document with his ring and stretches out his hand to pass it to the officer sitting opposite him. He waits for the receipt and so we see

in the palm of his hand the hint of the letter C.

The sound of gale-force wind.

Torn sails blown out by the force of it.

The prow of a ship looms up carried by the swell.

Dark forbidding rocks roam perilously near.

Lightning flashes as the mast cuts the sky.

Flames encircle the vessel and light up the night sky.

Somewhere in the bowels of the ship the convicts shouting and screaming. Then total darkness.

We can hear nothing of their cries for the torrent of wind and sea.

The burnt-out shell of the ship in the morning light.

The ship on the lantern-slide rocks to and fro, then gradually settles on a peaceful sea.

The image dissolves on a white sheet upstage in the Old Vic Theatre, London. We are looking on to the stage framed by the gilt proscenium. The Lanternist leaves his lectern for centre stage where he takes his bow. Applause. He now appears as an elegant figure holding his lecturer's stick, making a grandiloquent gesture before moving stage left. The applause changes gear for the oncoming Mr Pitt, entering from stage right, beaming with magnanimity. Before and above them are festoons of garlands and a banner declaring the words LONDON–DORCHESTER COMMITTEE: WELCOME

Mr Pitt waves his hands for quiet and addresses the assembly:

PITT: Ladies and gentlemen. It is my privilege to stand here as the representative of you all, many thousands of men and women from all parts of the country, whose prayers, entreaties and remonstrances have brought about the return of these ill-used men . . .

The applause becomes even more enthusiastic as he extends his hand for the Tolpuddle men and their families to come onstage. They progress to centre stage where six chairs wait in line. Brine, Young Stanfield, Old Stanfield, George and James Loveless take their seats. The sixth chair is empty. Behind the men, their respective families take up their places.

PITT: . . . and who supported their families during their long and arduous exile. I do not have to remind you that the women have suffered along with their men . . .

At close range, the families look awkward and modest in the limelight. We dwell on the tableau, and see that John Hammett and Bridget now have three small children standing behind the empty chair. In their embarrassment Betsy and Diana glance at one another gathering reassurance. The children – Hetty, Charity and Joseph – are a little more grown up and on their best behaviour. The only slight movement comes from Elvi who edges towards Brine and his mother. He and Young Stanfield have both acquired fashionable hairdos. The only physical contact comes from Sarah Loveless who has her arms around her husband's neck.

PITT: We should never forget the authors and abettors of this cruel and vindictive violation of the laws of humanity. Most truly those men have earned for themselves an ignoble fame! But my task today is to praise and thank those others who have helped our cause . . .

VOICES: Robert Owen . . . Hume . . . Cobbett . . . O'Connor . . . Hartwell . . . Wakley . . . William Morden Pitt . . .

Laughter.

PITT: Yes . . .

VOICE: Don't you be forgetting Lord John Russell.

Sounds of boos.

PITT: Let us give credit where it is due, for when that gentleman became Home Secretary he was finally persuaded to grant a full and free pardon.

129

Mr Pitt looks out into the auditorium.

PITT: But see who have really lent their weight to these joint
efforts. Silk Weavers ... Shipwrights ... Joiners ...
Cordwainers ... Journeymen Tailors ... Hatters ...
Caulkers ...

VOICES: (*Interspersed*) Farriers ... Whitesmiths ...
Bricklayers ... Blacksmiths ... Tinplate Workers ... Glass
Blowers ... Trimmers ... Wheelers ... Brushmakers ...

PITT: Yes, yes. Paper Stainers ... Coach Painters ... and
Gardeners. To all of you, our heartfelt thanks.

He turns to the Lanternist who has taken up a position at one
side of the group.

PITT: And finally, ladies and gentlemen, let us thank our
friend the Lanternist who, through the power of optics and its
magical transformations, has told the story here today.

The Lanternist takes a final deep bow.

PITT: It was almost as though he had been present
throughout himself.

The Lanternist looks conspiratorially direct at us.

PITT: *Ars magna lucis et ombrae*. George ...

As his speech comes to an end there are cheers. Mr Pitt is

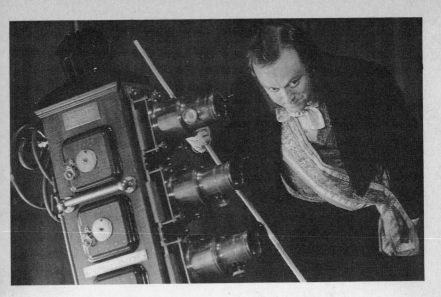

encouraging George to come forward. George appears to be somewhat reluctant. Perhaps he feels the occasion is best shared with others. But the sounds of banging chairs and feet force him to rise and he moves forward.

Then George is there in silence, isolated in a spotlight.

GEORGE: Comrades. I believe that God works by means and men. Under such an impression, I call upon every working man in England to shake off that supineness and indifference to their interests which leaves them in the situation of slaves. Has not the working man as much right to preserve and protect his labour as the rich man has his capital? Such a measure, I am well aware, would be dreaded, reviled and reprobated by the monied part of the nation: they would devise all those schemes, stratagems and policy that the art and cunning of man can invent to thwart and retard it. But let the working classes of Britain, seeing the necessity of acting upon such a principle, remembering that union is power, listen to nothing that might be presented before them to draw their attention from the subject, alike despising and conquering party disputes and personal bickerings; and they will accomplish their own salvation and that of the world.

The place has become deathly quiet. We can no longer see anything surrounding George. It is as if he stands on the edge of eternity.

GEORGE: Let every working man come forward, from east to west, from north to south; unite firmly but peaceably together as the heart of one man; then no longer would the interests of the millions be sacrificed for the gain of a few, but the blessings resulting from such a change would be felt by us and our posterity even to generations yet unborn.

Click-click.

We see a lantern slide portrait of George Loveless and the words:

> George Loveless
> Died in Canada aged 77

We hear the click-clicking sound of the lantern and see a portrait of James Loveless and the words:

> James Loveless
> Died in Canada aged 65

Again the click-click of the slide mechanism and the face of Old Stanfield:

> Thomas Stanfield
> Died in Canada aged 74

Click-click for Young Stanfield:

> John Stanfield
> Died in Canada aged 85

Click-click for Brine:

> James Brine
> Married Elvi Stanfield
> Died in Canada aged 90

And click-click for Hammett:

> James Hammett
> Survived and returned to Tolpuddle
> Married three times
> Died in Dorchester Workhouse aged 79

Finally there is Queen Victoria and the words:

> God Save The Queen

Click-click and we are left with a piercing white circle of light.

Comrades opened at the Curzon West End, London in August 1987.

THE CAST

Dorset

GEORGE LOVELESS	Robin Soans
BETSY LOVELESS	Imelda Staunton
HETTY LOVELESS	Amber Wilkinson
JAMES LOVELESS	William Gaminara
SARAH LOVELESS	Katy Behean
OLD TOM STANFIELD	Stephen Bateman
DIANA STANFIELD	Sandra Voe
YOUNG STANFIELD	Philip Davis
ELVI STANFIELD	Valerie Whittington
CHARITY STANFIELD	Harriet Doyle
JOHN HAMMETT	Patrick Field
BRIDGET HAMMETT	Heather Page
JAMES HAMMETT	Keith Allen
MRS BRINE	Patricia Healey
BRINE	Jeremy Flynn
JOSEPH BRINE	Shane Down
FRAMPTON	Robert Stephens
MRS FRAMPTON	Joanna David
PITT	Michael Hordern
VICAR	Freddie Jones
MRS WETHAM	Barbara Windsor
CLERK	Murray Melvin
GENTLEMAN FARMER	Trevor Ainsley
GENTLEMAN FARMER	Malcolm Terris
FOREMAN	Dave Atkins
SERVANT GIRL	Collette Barker
SAILOR	Michael Clark
GAOLER	Alex McCrindle
CONSTABLE	Jack Chissick
BLONDE GIRL	Sarah Reed
DARK GIRL	Nicola Hayward
LEGG	Mark Brown

Australia

MRS CARLYLE	Vanessa Redgrave
NORFOLK	James Fox
THE FOP	Arthur Dignam

THE CONVICT	John Hargreaves
CHARLIE	Symon Parsonage
LONE ABORIGINE	Charles Yunipingu
FLOWER	Simone Landis
WOMAN IN WHITE	Anna Volska
AUCTIONEER	Brian MacDermott
OFFICIAL AT BURIAL	Shane Briant
REGISTRAR	Tim Eliot
POLICE OFFICER	David Netheim
BERTIE THE GUARD	Ralph Cotterill
DIGGER	David McWilliams
WHORE	Lynette Curran

and

LANTERNIST, SERGEANT BELL, MR WETHAM,
DIORAMA SHOWMAN, LAUGHING CAVALIER, USHER,
WOLLASTON, RANGER, TRAMP, CAPTAIN, McCALLUM,
SILHOUETTIST, MAD PHOTOGRAPHER, WITCH
Alex Norton

Director/Writer	Bill Douglas
Producer	Simon Relph
Associate Producers	David Hannay
	Redmond Morris
Production Managers	Donna Grey
	Charles Hannah
Production Co-Ordinator	Deborah Carter
Lighting Cameraman/Operator	Gale Tattersall
Stills Photographer	David Appleby
Composers	Hans Werner Henze
	David Graham
Costume Designers	Doreen Watkinson
	Bruce Finlayson
Make-Up Artist	Elaine Carew
Production Designer	Michael Pickwoad
Film Editor	Mick Audsley
Script Editor	Peter Jewell

Comrades is a Skreba production in association with National Film
Finance Corporation, Film Four International and Curzon Film
Distributors.